PITCH A WITCH

MAYA DANIELS

vinci BOOKS

By Maya Daniels

Chronicles of Forbidden Witchery

Resting Witch Face
Pitch a Witch
Witch Please
Payback is a Witch

Vinci Books

vinci-books.com

Published by Vinci Books Ltd in 2025

1

Copyright © Maya Daniels 2021

The author has asserted their moral right to be identified as the author of this work in accordance with the Copyright, Designs and Patents Act 1988. This work is a work of fiction. Names, characters, places and incidents are the product of the author's imagination or are used fictitiously. Any resemblance to actual persons, living or dead, places and incidents is entirely coincidental.
All rights reserved. No part of this publication may be copied, reproduced, distributed, stored in any retrieval system, or transmitted in any form or by any means, including photocopying, recording, or other electronic or mechanical methods, nor used as a source for any form of machine learning including AI datasets, without the prior written permission of the publisher.
The publisher and the author have made every effort to obtain permissions for any third party material used in this book and to comply with copyright law. Any queries in this respect should be brought to the attention of the publisher and any omissions will be corrected in future editions.
A CIP catalogue record for this book is available from the British Library.
Paperback ISBN: 9781036705794

Chapter One

"No." That one word stung like a slap across my face.

Bristling at the blatant refusal, my arms folded across my chest like they had a mind of their own. Standing in Alex Greywood's home office was not my favorite pastime on the worst of days, but it was a solid plan to get my ass out of pack lands and back where I belonged. Unfortunately, I had to act like a ten-year-old having a tantrum, but a girl had to do what a girl had to do.

"They"—Speaking slowly and deliberately, I narrowed my eyes at the alpha, who was scowling down his nose at me — "owe me a Mercedes SLK55. It's a convertible, might I remind you. I have every right to demand they compensate me for my way-over-one-hundred-thousand-dollar car ... in person." My forefinger snapped at his face like a whip on that last part.

With a tortured groan that made me think the conversation was causing him physical pain, Alex shook his head at me. "I know how much that car costs, Hazel, but we need to deal with the vampires delicately, as you well know. We can't demand anything if we are trying to convince them not to amalgamate with the demons and to leave you alone. It's your life we are talking about here, woman. You must work with me on this."

"Tell that to my poor car. They pulverized it, Alex." Widening my peepers to get my point across better, I slammed my fist on his desk for emphasis. We both knew this had nothing to do with the vehicle or how much it cost since that was small potatoes for Danika's bank account, but the great person he was, the alpha played along with it ... for the moment.

"Pulverized it." His mouth twisted as if me repeating that fact was a foul stench drifting up his nose while I grinded my fist into the palm of my other hand to add a visual experience. "As in smashed it like it owed them a life debt. Its guts were sprinkled all over the road, too. You can check it out for yourself if you don't believe me, since it's used as a scarecrow in the middle of a freaking cornfield now."

A soft click announced the door of the office opening, and Amber poked her head inside, brightening the moment her eyes landed on her mate. He dropped the glower as well, turning his body toward her like she was the sun in his solar system and he gravitated toward it subconsciously. It was always as disgusting as it was fascinating to see how much these two loved each other. And I meant disgusting in the sweetest possible way. Anyone around them wished to find a connection like that, but rarely anyone got lucky enough to experience it.

One thing I knew for sure was I'd never find that in my lifetime.

"I can come back later if you two are busy," Amber addressed Alex, but her warm smile was aimed at me.

I curled the corners of my lips tightly in return, fighting the need to squirm. I adored the redhead more than anyone else and didn't deserve her kindness. With her presence, my plan to get back to my house had gone down the drain, however. Guilt drilled a hole in my stomach from the thought.

"No, no. Please come in, my love. Maybe you can talk some sense into her," Alex huffed, waving a hand toward me as if there was another idiot standing inside his office with us and he needed to point out who he was talking about. "She's as stubborn as any other female in this house. It's like talking to a brick wall. Are we absolutely certain she's not a shifter?"

"Why is it that I'm being called stubborn for refusing to let them get away with constantly causing unnecessary damage to others?" Turning from Alex to Amber, I raised my eyebrows all the way to my hairline. "Do you know what I've had to sacrifice because of demons and vampires lately? Do you?"

"Is this about the boots, again? I swear to the full moon I will start howling if I hear one more thing about shoes or clothing," the alpha snarled at me, his finger pointed accusingly at my face.

Amber snickered, stepping inside and closing the door. I watched her from the corner of my eye as she moved to join him behind the long wooden desk while I continued my argument, disregarding the little tid-bit that I was an adult woman and not a snotty child.

"They were designer boots, as I've pointed out many times. You are a guy, so of course you don't sympathize with my pain on that matter." My pout made a muscle twitch under his green eye. The blue one shot daggers at me. "I just bought them, too." Was I acting like a sullen toddler? Why, yes. Yes, I was.

"Sit down, love." Amber patted her mate on the chest and, none too gently, shoved him in the leather chair. He huffed and narrowed his gaze on her but wisely stayed silent. "We don't want you to burst a blood vessel while Hazel here is trying to find a way to leave pack lands."

"What ... I ... I would never." Stuttering and acting appalled at the accusations, I made the mistake of laying it on too thick. "I'm not dumb to leave when I'm safe and protected here."

I winced.

I should've just stopped at "never."

Damn it.

"Like you didn't try to sneak out yesterday when the patrol found you trying to hot-wire one of the vehicles?" Amber giggled good-naturedly, but a storm darkened her mate's face as his eyes drilled holes in my face from across the desk.

My mouth opened and closed, yet nothing came out of it. Admitting defeat was never easy for me, but I had it on good authority that this battle wouldn't be won if what I knew about Alex Greywood was true. Not at that moment anyway. So, shrewdly I shrugged and toed the edge of the rug with my shoe like a teenager. It was painful to see my master plan backfire.

"If I say I was testing how effective your beta's teams were when on patrol, would you believe me?" With a syrupy smile plastered on my face, I mockingly fluttered my eyelashes at the alpha. I was going out of my freaking mind. He knew it, I knew it, and the entire fucking pack knew I was ready to peel off my own skin from frustration.

Instead of shouting, reprimanding, or even kicking me

out as any other person with a brain would've done in his place after my obnoxious behavior, Alex slouched in the chair with a sigh. "Why?" was all he asked, and it came out in a low, even tone while he rubbed a hand over his face.

"It's been eight days, nine hours, and thirty-four minutes, Alex. No one has returned with any answers or a fucking solution to my little problem here." His arched eyebrow chafed at me badly.

Not even Amber shaking her head at me in disappointment could change the fact that I was miserable enough to risk death just so I could join Sissily out there. I missed my friend more than anything else, although she probably hated my guts after seeing what kind of a freak I was.

"Yes, I've been counting, damn it. You would be, too, if you had to hide like a coward while everyone you care about is risking their life out there."

"Who are you and what did you do to Hazel?" Astonished, I gaped as he peered at me with a small smile playing at the corners of his mouth.

It took my brain a moment to register that he'd joked to lessen the tension radiating from me. Ever since I was deposited on his doorstep like some unwanted offspring, I worked hard daily to learn about the unexpected magic I suddenly had. Be it with Amber in the mornings where she did everything to make me comfortable with all the emotional changes happening inside my body, or with a multitude of shifters, including their alpha, to keep me in top physical shape so I didn't succumb to my powers. I still felt trapped, no matter what little progress I'd made or whatever fun I had, by the fact I was no longer a dud.

I gave him a flat, unimpressed look.

"I understand how you feel, I really do," Alex expressed with a measured tone, and Amber hummed in agreement from where she was perched comfortably on his lap. Good thing she sat on him because I had no doubt he would jump over the desk and strangle me otherwise. "It's never easy to sit back while others take control of the wheel, but this is only temporary. The deeper we dig into what is going on with the demons, the more invested I am as well. All this frustration because you think you're not doing anything is just the calm before the storm. I've seen it more times than I can count."

"I'm losing my mind, Alex." My nails scraped my scalp harshly as I started pacing. "Danika is in her own world playing a dictator and making sure everyone dances to her tune, but the truth of the matter is, all of you are in danger because of me. Call me an idiot, but I'm not going to sit and be obedient just to make her or anyone else happy. I should be out there figuring this out with everyone else."

Mismatched eyes rolled over me with a calculating glint that did not bode well for me. After Danika dropped a shit ton of bombs in this very office, she took Blondie and my best friend, and I had yet to hear a word from any of them. River staying away from me was a great thing. I didn't trust the pretty boy now any more than I did the first time I'd laid eyes on him. All my girly parts were having a blast from him being around, though my trust issues slapped that nonsense away fast enough, thank Hecate. But Sissily? I needed to talk to her. To apologize for what I was, or for my incompetence to control the magic I never knew I had. To tell her something.

Anything really.

I felt lost, and more than anything, I was afraid I'd lost the only person who always had my back no matter how bad things turned out. Each night since she walked out the door and left me behind without saying a word, her fearful expression had haunted my nightmares. I'd live with everyone hating me, or even being made fun of by every witch in existence. I just wanted my friend back.

"I'll make you a deal." Alex waited while I struggled to inflate my lungs. "If no one comes to give us news by Friday, I'm taking you with me to pay your coven a visit."

It was Monday morning.

"By Wednesday." Holding his gaze, I countered, doing everything in my power not to gnaw on my lip when the full power of an alpha stare stabbed my pupils.

With a chuckle, he planted a kiss on Amber's shoulder, then grinned at me. "You fit perfectly in this house. Thursday, and not a day sooner."

"I feel wonderful that I need to resort to childish behavior so I can do what's right, just so you know." Grimacing, I turned toward the door, eager to leave before I died from embarrassment.

"Not that fast, dear." Amber's voice made me pause with one hand on the doorknob, the door opened just a crack. "As you said, it's been eight days, and you are yet to cook with me."

"I knew something was going to bite me in the ass from this conversation, I just didn't know what." Beaming at her when she giggled, I waited by the open door for her to join me.

"We have a pack gathering this evening, so we better get started."

Alex guffawed at my horrified expression. His barking laughter followed us to the kitchen like a theme song announcing our entrance inside a fight ring.

Chapter Two

"Hazel made those cupcakes," Amber announced loud enough for everyone present to hear, and I winced. "Aren't they scrumptious?"

Their home was packed to the brim.

Every single member of the pack was in attendance for what turned out to be a pack party, and they spilled from the house to fill every space available on the lawn as well. Until an hour before that, I had successfully managed to avoid most that were not involved in my training, especially Alex's beta Ace. Ace and I had a thing back when—okay, fine, we had tons of hot, mind-blowing sex—after which I'd tucked tail and never returned his calls, thinking playing possum was the best way to run from situations involving emotions. We'd not come face to face since then, and I made a valid effort to open the ground so it could swallow me whole when his sharp, intense gaze snapped in my direction. Unfortunately, although I now had magic, the damn shit did not work in my favor—not that morning when I'd acted like an idiot with his alpha, and it didn't do jack shit now, either.

"They are magical, Mom." Stella, Amber's oldest daughter, hip-bumped me. "Get it? Magical." Her snickering should've helped ease my freak-out mode, but it did not.

Stella was fifteen years old and a replica of her mother. From the fire-red corkscrews dancing around her shoulders to her sweet face with those large, expressive eyes and a ready smile for everyone who met her gaze. Her young body had developed curves early, which was distinctive for shifter women, and a few boys were already circling around her like moons in orbit. We'd spent a lot of time together while I was stuck in my voluntary exile, and her familiarity calmed my nerves somewhat.

"It's shocking that a witch can make such delicious sweets," I groused, thickly layering the sarcasm in my tone and playfully glaring at Amber. "You should've said it louder, though. I'm not sure they heard you in Cleveland." We beamed at each other, but the little joy I had died a sudden death.

"Incoming," Stella mumbled from the corner of her mouth, but I didn't have the opportunity to say a word in reply.

"Hey, kiddo. Evening, Amber," Ace addressed the other two women, although he had his dark eyes pinned on me. "Hazel."

"Ace," I croaked uncomfortably.

Amber frowned, glancing between us before focusing her full attention on the beta wolf. "Ace, so nice that you found the time to join us." She greeted him warmly and gave him a hug. "Alex wasn't sure you'd make it with all the organizing he's been forking on your plate lately. He will be ecstatic to see you."

What was the point in having magic if I couldn't make myself disappear when needed? Stella, the teenager that she was, dug her short nails into the skin on the inside of my upper arm, practically vibrating from the anticipation of drama. Yes, I dumbly might've mentioned the beta to the girl. I was bored out of my mind unless I was training and couldn't be held accountable for what came out of my mouth.

Magic or not, I needed to be put down. Stat.

"The teams already made the routes a routine. I'm just assuring the effectiveness of the pairing now. Besides, I always have time for your food." The shifter was charming, I'd give him that much.

At around six feet, give or take an inch, Ace was a wall of solid muscle perfectly wrapped in sun-kissed skin. Light brown hair in a military cut only emphasized his sharp, rakishly handsome features instead of dampening them, which it would've done to most men, but I liked a guy with some hair on his head for ... well, I'd leave the rest unsaid. My stomach seemed to be remembering him a little too well, too, because it was perfecting the art of flipflopping while I looked at everything but the wolf. The reminder that he was actually in charge of making sure the pack lands were not breached by whoever wanted me dead made me feel smaller than a speckle of dust.

Awkward didn't cover it.

"Talking about food, you must try Hazel's cupcakes, Ace." I almost swallowed my tongue when Amber beamed at the beta. His gaze darkened as it bore into mine, and I gave my best attempt at impersonating a deer in headlights while trying to slow the galloping of my heart.

Why me?

"Oh, yeah, Mom. He simply muuusssssstt try Hazel's cupcakes." Stella chortled and wiggled her eyebrows. I wanted to kill the kid. "They are yummy." Clinging to my arm, she giggled so hard she snorted and slapped her hand over her mouth.

My face was on fire.

"Stella, manners," Amber chastised her daughter sternly. "I swear she was the sweetest girl only yesterday." The older woman shook her head at the beta. "One day they are sweet and adorable, and the next they are insubordinate little gremlins that feed on your soul."

Ace chuckled seeing Amber's grimace but winked at Stella when she gasped in outrage at her mother's comment. I made a half-hearted attempt at laughing, but it sounded forced even to my own ears. It was cut short when the young girl stormed away from where we were standing on the outside patio, and Amber rushed after her with an apologetic look thrown my way.

"Kids." I snickered awkwardly, wishing I was anywhere else but on that patio with this particular man.

"It's nice to see you again, Hazel." Ace didn't waste time and spoke in a tone charged with accusation.

If I'd been a fair person, I had no reason to dislike the guy. He never did anything I didn't encourage, and then some. Honestly, his only fault had been that he'd wanted more than I was emotionally ready to offer at the time. Plus, fairness had nothing to do with the situation I found myself in anyway.

"Is it, though?" Finally meeting his eyes, I smiled thinly. "Hit me with it, Ace. Now is your chance to pour out everything you didn't get a chance to say."

"Coward." I jerked at the calmness in that one word.

"What?"

"You heard me." Stepping close enough that his cologne surrounded me in a cloud of fresh citrus, he looked down at me through a half-lidded stare. "I said you are a coward, Hazel Byrne."

"O-kay then." Grappling with my heartbeat in the hope not to sound breathless, I cocked my hip and speared him with a fierce glare. "Insults it is, then. Let's see what else you've got, big man. I'm as ready as I'll ever be."

With a sigh, he stepped back but reached out to tuck a strand of hair behind my ear. I stiffened. "I apologize. It's not my intention to make you uncomfortable, Hazel. The reasons that made you disappear on me are your own, and I don't want that to be the cause of you avoiding me while you are here."

"It's not like I didn't deserve it." Mumbling because all the fight drained out of me, I answered his slight smile with one of my own. "But if you remember, I did tell you I'm an ass the day we met."

"That you did." Chuckling, he relaxed the stiffness in his shoulders, which had escaped my notice until that moment.

Probably because the white t-shirt he had on stuck to him like its life depended on it, outlining every sculpted line of muscle on his torso. I might freely admit that I was an ass, but I was not a blind ass. The shifter was stunning, and what was worse was he knew it.

"How are you holding up?" Typical Ace, he cared more about everyone's comfort than his own. Including mine, though he should've flipped me off the moment he saw me and walked away.

"It's a dream come true, let me tell ya. I'm having a blast." With a sigh, I followed him to the coolers filled with ice so we could grab drinks, too aware of the heat of his palm on my lower back.

"That bad, huh?" The rumble in his chest as he chuckled softly sounded familiar and put me at ease.

I never understood why he always found me funny, but every single time he laughed, I liked it very much. I would've loved having Ace as a friend because he was one of the good ones, but I'd screwed that up when I helped him take off his pants. Not that I had something against staying friends when things didn't work out, but as soon as emotions got involved, friendship bought a one-way ticket out of town. I was a self-confessed bitch, but I'd never be so cruel to play with a person's feelings.

"Sitting on my ass while others may be in danger never sat well with me." Accepting the beer bottle he offered, I clinked it off his before taking a small sip. "I'm in much better shape now than ever before, yet all I do is practice ... and bake cupcakes, apparently."

"Very good cupcakes, according to Amber." His smile slipped, and he moved closer to keep the conversation between us. "I agree with Alex that you should stay for now. So far, we have three to four attempts to enter the pack's grounds daily, Hazel. The first couple of days, it was just vampires and one or two brave bastards from the Blackwood pack. Lately, we've also been adding demons to the body count."

My breath got stuck in my windpipe like a fist had been jammed there. My chest tightened painfully as I searched for a way to convey how that made me feel. In the end, I realized there were no words I could find to express the impotence strangling my soul from the fact that those gunning for my head would never stop. They'd just keep coming until everyone I knew or cared about was dead.

"That is actually a very good reason why I shouldn't be here, Ace." His mouth opened, but I silenced him with a raised hand. "No, hear me out. If the roles were reversed and you knew people here would get hurt eventually because of you, would you stay?"

Silence stretched while he held me trapped in his bottomless stare.

"I didn't think so." Playfully, I tapped his arm with the bottle clutched in my hand. "So, what are we going to do about it?"

"We?" Ace stepped back and took a long swig from his beer. "Ten minutes ago, you didn't want to be on the same planet as me, and now we are doing things? Together?"

His dark gaze rolled over me, stopping longer than was polite in a few places. Where my neck met my shoulder, around my boobs, which were peeking from the open buttons of my deep purple silky blouse, and mostly around my hips where I stood angled between him and the house at my back. As a shifter, Ace obviously paid closest attention to the lower part of my body. He was a butt man, through and through, and shamelessly I took advantage of the attraction he still had for me.

"I need to get out of here without Alex dragging me back kicking and screaming," I pointed out the obvious, shifting sideways more so he had a better view of my ass. "You know where each patrol is at any given time and how to accomplish that without your alpha or his mate knowing I'm gone. And before you start lecturing me, let me say one thing: I don't want to die. I just couldn't live with myself if someone else does. I have to do something."

"And what is the something that you want to do, Hazel?" His eyes were glued to what he could see of my perky butt, but at least he didn't give me a resounding no, so I rushed to further my case.

"I just want to see what is happening with my coven, my grandmother, and my friend. You know. Just an adventure of reconnaissance. They won't even know I'm there."

"I don't think a reality exists where people don't know you are there, Hazel." Ace's lips curled in a telling smirk that I pointedly ignored.

"You going to help me or not?" I deadpanned, done playing stupid games with the beta. Ace was handsome, but not enough for me to talk in circles all night. Couldn't he see the shit I had to do and how important it was?

"You knew I'd help before you even asked." There was no accusation or frustration in his statement.

"Right, I just had to stroke your ego so you would free me into the world, huh?" The weight pressing on my chest lifted somewhat, so my comment held no bite.

Amber finally emerged from the house, and as soon as her gaze found me, she headed our way. My smile was genuine and a lot less strained while I waited for her to join us.

"I said I'd help you, not set you free." Ace snorted like I was dumb or something.

"Huh?" Amber was almost to where we stood at the side of the porch.

"No way you are getting loose. I'm going with you, Hazel."

Fuck a duck!

Chapter Three

"There was absolutely no need for you to tag along," I grumbled the next night, folding my arms across my chest as I glared out the window of Ace's SUV.

What was it with the damn shifters and their four-wheel drives anyway? None of them would be caught dead in anything other than a SUV. This one smelled like the beta mixed with the scent of freshly-cut grass, and I sank deeper into the buttery soft leather of the passenger seat so I didn't bite his head off when he snorted at my annoyance. A metal chain dangled from the rearview mirror with the head of a wolf swinging between us like a pendulum, compliments of the bumpy road we were on. Gravel crunched under the thick tires, and trees blurred in my vision as we flew away from the pack lands illuminated only by the headlights of the car.

"There was no need, you are correct. There was a want, however." The infuriating man kept snickering like everything was a joke to him.

"I'm perfectly capable of taking care of myself, Ace."

With a dramatic huff, I wiggled in my seat so I could face him, but the stupid seatbelt was trying to choke me, for Hecate's sake. "You of all people should know this."

It was the truth.

The night I met Ace was anything but a usual encounter where two people meet each other and later become ... something. Sissily and I were flopping around the dance floor like fish out of water, giggling like schoolgirls after a dozen cocktails, when a warm, large hand folded over my arm. In my typical fashion, instead of turning to see who it was, I took hold of the offending appendage, tilted my pelvis forward, and flipped him over my shoulder. Ace dropped like a rock at my feet with a loud humph from all the air pushing out of his lungs. We exchanged names while I'd loomed over the beta as he'd stretched out on his back in the middle of the club and grinned like a loon up at me.

"You asked me to go against my alpha and I agreed to do it, Hazel." All humor gone, he side-eyed me and tightened his hold on the steering wheel. "This way, at least I can save face by claiming I was with you the whole time when he chews me up because I contravened his orders."

Since I had nothing to say to that, I kept my mouth shut as we bumped along the road, my organs rearranging themselves from the dips and larger rocks we hit. Ace was right. Instead of giving him a hard time for shadowing me, I should be grateful he'd entertained my crazy idea to sneak me out in the first place. The problem I had was the unease accompanying the clawing fear that had rattled my bones the moment I jumped in the car, which I was trying very hard to hide. After the mad chase we had through the city over a week ago and the Blackwood shifters pushing me off the road in the middle of a cornfield, I hadn't stepped foot outside of the pack's land, which was practically vacuum sealed with guards patrolling day and night.

Ace eased off the gas pedal and slowed the breakneck speed when we entered the outskirts of the city. Too soon, buildings replaced the open fields and traffic surged from all sides. What I'd hoped would be relief at finding myself back where everything was familiar had turned into panic-induced anxiety that sent hot-cold flashes through my body. Heart palpitations shortened my breath, and cold sweat dampened the back of my shirt. My eyes darted left and right when I saw the ominous shadows reaching for my soul and looming everywhere I turned. I worked hard to keep my emotional state calm and collected so my magic wouldn't surge up and cause a distraction, but it was a real struggle at that moment.

A soft, golden glow melded with the blue light emanating from the dashboard, alerting me that my power was about to make an appearance. Hurriedly, I stabbed my hands under my light jacket, which I had draped over my thighs so I could hide the symbols coming to life all over my skin. Glamour or not, I needed to ensure that nobody saw me impersonating a glow stick in Ace's car, so I eyed him to see if he had any reaction to it. Appeased that Danika knew her shit well, I slumped in the seat and took slow, measured breaths until I was calm. Well, as calm as I could be given my predicament.

"Are we stopping at the Gatekeeper's Coven?" Ace took Superior Avenue past the Casino pulsing with bright lights, only slowing at the stoplights. "We can conduct reconnaissance first if you'd like and turn back after we are sure everything is good."

"I'm not hiding from my coven, Ace. Just from Danika," I muttered, embarrassed that even as an adult I feared my grandmother. The witch was a shark, and if the beta had any common sense at all, he wouldn't want to come face to face with her either.

We turned right on 6th Street, crawling to the end of it before making a second right to double back to the main road bisecting Cleveland. Chomping on the inside of my mouth, I debated my options. When we passed a store selling mystical thingamajigs, I smacked the wolf's arm with the back of my hand.

"Park there." Enthusiastically, I stabbed my finger in the direction of an empty spot on the side of the street.

Ace arched an eyebrow but did what he was told like the smart man he was. The store was a tiny little thing but only a block from my coven, which happened to work perfectly for what I had in mind. The seatbelt hissed like a snake when I yanked it off me, and I jumped out the moment the SUV glided next to the sidewalk.

"What are we doing here?" Ace asked as he slapped the driver's door closed.

I was already wiggling my fingers in the back pocket of my high-waisted baggy jeans, which I'd paired with a Prada bralette top that gave me a cute skater look that was still very feminine thanks to the silver Louboutin pumps I had on. The light denim jacket matched it perfectly, too. Skinny jeans were so last season, and breaking up with them was one of the best fashion choices I'd made in a while.

"Shopping." Grinning like a mad woman, I flicked my black credit card at his face. "Come on, it'll be fun. We will investigate, plus we will get ourselves lots of goodies. What do you say?"

"I say I've never met a female who loves spending money the way you do." The shifter smiled enigmatically and shook his head at me. "Far be it for me to stand between you and a store. I'm not that brave."

"You're hoping that I'll get so engrossed in pretties that I'll forget about sneaking inside the coven, don't you?" Laughing at the sheepish grin tugging on his mouth, I looped my arm through his as soon as he rounded the car and dragged him down the sidewalk. "I can totally multitask."

"Do your thing, and I'll keep an eye on everything else." His dark eyes twinkled when he glanced at me, and a sharp pang stabbed me in the chest.

Maybe this was a bad idea.

All my justifications sounded lame when hope flashed in his irises. The way his body tilted toward me and his warm hand covered mine where I gripped his forearm, or how his smile seemed brighter, flirtier, all of it screamed at me to stop being an ass and hide inside the car. But that meant going back to pack lands where there was no Sissily. There was a special place in hell for those like me, that much I knew.

"You are awesome, Ace." Instead of turning back, I beamed at him while guilt drilled a hole in my stomach.

You are doing it for Sissily. She'd do the same for you. No matter how many times I repeated it, it didn't make me feel better. If I had a brain, I would've called my friend and asked her to meet us or even visit the alpha's house. Stubbornly, I waited for her to call, which didn't happen. Hurting Ace again only added another stain on my soul—one I wouldn't be able to wash out.

The next hour or so, I dragged the shifter from store to store, piling his arms with bags and drowning in misery every time he laughed or whistled when I tried something on. To appease my guilt, I showered him with gifts too, for which he protested loudly. No amount of explaining that it was for him helping to keep me sane stopped his grumbling, but I did it anyway.

In the last store, I perched him in the chair in front of the dressing rooms and told him I'd like to try on one of the dresses. After I picked one that would look more appropriate on a prostitute than anyone else and made sure he waited with anticipation to see me in it, I ducked out of the store and left him behind. I was at the end of the block, my heels tapping a staccato rhythm over the sidewalk when I heard his roar.

"Hazel!" Ace's shout bellowed down the street, and I winced.

Fuck my life. Now the whole city knew I was there. Jumping from one foot to the other, I yanked my Louboutins off, and clutching them in both hands, I hightailed it toward the coven.

Chapter Four

The coven building loomed above me like a menacing beast when I reached the marble stairs that would lead me to the front doors. Half of the domed roof was still caved in from my fiasco in the library, and one side of the obsidian wall was in shambles.

Hysterical laughter bubbled out of my chest when I looked at the keys above the double doors, their red color like a splash of blood over the black stone. One was dangling crookedly while it fought gravity, one was missing, and the third was half visible, the rest covered in soot and dust. If Hecate hadn't been pissed at me before I blew the coven up, she sure as hell would be now.

A few cars were parked in the parking lot on my left.

"It's now or never, Hazel." A deranged snicker rasped out of my throat, and I stretched my legs as far as I could to reach the building faster, my bare feet slapping the marble since I was clutching the silver pumps in my hands like spiked dumbbells used for exercise.

All my hopes rested on my best friend being inside the building.

The glow on my skin, which had diminished while shopping, burst into existence the closer I got to the sizeable entrance. The short hairs on my neck prickled with awareness, alerting me that someone was watching my progress, so I redoubled my efforts. Working out with the shifters had helped for something, at least, though I had a feeling Ace was gaining on me.

Someone shouted when I crashed through the front doors and sent him flying to the opposite sides of the walls before he ducked away from the long hallway. Shock speared through me. How was I capable of doing that when usually the doors were heavy enough to require a full-body shove to nudge them a few inches?

My arms pumped as I flew toward the only place I thought my friend would visit, ignoring the black candles with their unmoving blue flames. As soon as I took a turn to reach the training facilities, voices echoed behind me, lighting a fire under my butt. Whoever I'd startled with my not-so-subtle entrance had called reinforcements.

Secretly, I hoped it was Sasha Airborne they sent after me.

The training room was empty.

I doubled over, panting and clutching my Louboutin pumps to my chest while tears burned the back of my eyes. Mats were pushed to one side, and the standing punching bags were clustered in another corner. Debris sat in a couple of piles with brooms leaned on the wall next to them. Just another reminder of what I'd done to the coven.

I wanted to cry. Dumb really, but there you had it.

Behind me, the door banged open when whoever had

given chase finally caught up to me. He panted heavily, too, but didn't say a word when I straightened and, without turning to face him, proceeded to put my shoes back on. Sweat glistened on my skin, and I wanted to peel the jacket off me, but I didn't.

"Miss Byrne, we didn't expect you here anytime soon." The nasal tone had me grinding my molars instantly.

"High Priest Shadowblood, how very nice to see you up and about." I turned his way, cocking an eyebrow at the old man. "How's the noggin? Still ticking, I see." I rapped my knuckles over my own skull for demonstration.

As always, hatred burned in his beady eyes, and I could've sworn all the shadows around us pulsed in sync with the fluttering vein on his neck. I zeroed-in on it, and my magic surged as if sensing a tasty treat. Clenching my fists until my nails bit into the skin of my palms, I shoved it down like Amber had taught me and smiled at him.

There was nothing pleasant in the curl of my mouth, and he answered it by showing more teeth than any mouth had the right to have.

"It'll take more than a building falling on top of me to kill me, Miss Byrne." He sneered, his upper lip trembling when it rose above his bared teeth. His thin, narrow face had the usual pinch, making me think my very existence disgusted him. And it probably did.

"You sound like you are accusing me of attempted murder, pops." Stepping closer to him, I regretted slipping my pumps back onto my feet. I could've nailed him with the heel if he kept talking shit out of his nonexistent ass. "If I wanted you to meet Hecate in person, I had no reason to try to kill myself in the process. I can snuff out your life with one hand tied behind my back." Grinning like a deranged person, I cocked my head at him and purred, "Wanna see?"

"Hazel Byrne."

Shadowblood preened when my grandmother's voice boomed from down the long hallway. I involuntarily flinched, which I bet made his day. Danika's power pelted my skin already, and that on its own told me that I was royally screwed. Not that I had any intentions of showing the weasel that.

Much to my surprise, although my grandmother could appear at any time, Shadowblood raised his hand and pointed his forefinger straight at my chest, a tendril of dark shadow curling from it until it stretched, moving in my direction.

I stiffened.

A manic glint entered his pitch-black gaze, and leering, he hunched forward, pushing his magic faster my way. Creeped out and maybe a little scared that he would provoke the power inside me to destroy what was left of our temple, I took a step back with a gasp.

The old man thought I was afraid of him, and his grimace twisted with glee that radiated from him in waves. I felt his magic collecting around the tip of his finger ready to attack, much to my surprise. I'd never felt it before, and it only added to my unease. Tensing, I lifted my hands in the hopes to stop him when a voice from behind me made my knees buckle.

"I don't think that's wise, Mr. Shadowblood." River's smooth baritone made me shiver for an entirely different reason. "I will kill you faster than you can finish that spell. Put your hand down."

How in all the hells-balls did he show up in the middle of the training facility? Apart from the priest and me, no one else was there until Blondie spoke. If I hadn't seen it with my own eyes, I never would've believed he could appear or disappear the same way Danika had when she pulled the trick in the cornfield over a week ago.

Yet, there he stood in all his golden glory, gifting the High Priest with his megawatt smile like he hadn't just told the loser he could end his pathetic life.

"Where did you come from?" Shadowblood hissed, but he dropped his hand limply. "She's not supposed to be here. I should've known you had something to do with it, Blackman."

River's bored expression said more than any words could.

The oppressive tension drenching the air lifted immediately when Danika swooped through the doorway and joined our little unexpected get together, nearly plowing Shadowblood over in her haste. Her cold, emerald stare stabbed me in the brain, and almost every thought I had running rampant there was silenced. All I could do was wonder why I thought this was a great idea. It sure felt that way when I'd left the beta in that dressing room back at the store.

Speaking of the wolf, Ace stuck his head in right behind my grandmother.

"I found them frolicking here." Shadowblood sniffed disdainfully.

All of us ignored him.

"Why are you here, Hazel?" Danika dismissed the weasel in order to try and kill me with a look. It was fascinating to watch the High Priest creep behind her, his sneer visible over her left shoulder.

Images of crows circled in my mind's eye.

"I was shopping and figured I'd stop to say hi." Baring my teeth, I smoothed a few strands of hair that had been sticking to the side of my face. "Hi, Danika. Long time no see. How're things going around here? Missing someone? Your granddaughter maybe?"

Her eye twitched.

"Let us go to my office."

Without waiting for anyone, she swirled around, her midnight black ponytail snapping like a whip as she stormed out of sight. Shadowblood rushed after her like the loser he was, which left me standing between River and Ace.

A rabbit between two foxes.

The weight of their calculating stares was unbearable.

"Well." Clapping my hands, I beamed at them in turn. Ace calling me a coward flashed in my head. "You heard her. Chop-chop, before she decides none of us are worth her time."

The sound of my pumps smacking the smooth floor bounced off the walls when I hightailed it after my grandmother. She was the lesser of two evils in my miserable life, after all.

What that said about my life choices, I had no idea.

Annoyed that I avoided confrontation when a week ago I would've jumped on the opportunity with gusto, I stifled the disappointment that Sissily was not present. Two sets of eyes followed me from a few feet away, and I almost barked out a laugh when I heard Ace's muttering.

"I've been chasing her halfway around the city until five minutes ago," the wolf grumbled under his breath. "You had no time for frolicking." When I glanced over my shoulder, I found River smirking at the beta.

"You'd be surprised what I can do in five, wolf." Blondie's deep voice vibrated inside my belly, and I really wanted to slap him. Ace's low growl only made the infuriating jerk chuckle.

"Move," I snapped, so frustrated I hastened my steps while still managing to glare daggers at both.

River threw his head back and laughed.

Lesson 8: *Stay away from pretty faces. They're not worth the toll on your sanity.*

Chapter Five

"Do you understand how idiotic this is?" Danika planted both her hands on the polished desk in her office and stared at me through furious eyes.

With a tired sigh, I stomped to the chair right in front of her and plopped on it with a groan. The torture device bit into my spine, and I pressed my mouth hard so I didn't yelp. With the adrenaline gone, I felt my muscles screaming at me for some reason, too. After all the training I'd done, I thought I had more stamina.

"Which part?" All four of them gaped at me like I was something they'd never seen before. In order not to meet Danika's penetrating gaze, I twisted my foot so I could look at the heel of my silver pump. "The shopping or the frolicking?"

My heart skipped a beat when I found a dark smudge on the silver shoe, but I breathed easier when it wiped off after I rubbed my thumb on it. I was seriously considering sending the demons an invoice to compensate me for everything of mine that they'd destroyed, intentional or not. I wondered if they'd ask for original receipts for the items.

"Are you listening?" My grandmother tilted her head in a very bird-like manner that unnerved me.

"I'll tell you what's idiotic, Grandmother. How about that?" Planting both my feet on the floor, I leaned forward and pressed my forearms on her desk, which brought us closer than I would've liked. "When you drop the bomb of …" Her startled gaze darting sideways had my voice trailing off.

Without looking away from her, I noticed Shadowblood practically salivating behind her shoulder, so I swallowed everything I wanted to throw at her face. "… not wanting me around anymore because of a nasty accident, I'd say that's idiotic. Why can't I help fix things up?"

Good save on my part, but the fact that Danika didn't trust the High Priest was a new development. Not that they had to be best buds and share all their secrets or anything before, but if she didn't feel free to talk in front of him, why was he in the office to begin with? I hoped that my raised eyebrows conveyed my puzzlement.

It didn't.

Shocking, I knew.

"You were hurt, Hazel. It's okay to take time to heal. I appreciate your dedication to make amends, but your health is more important." Her hand reached for mine, but before she could touch me, I yanked my arm back.

Danika's emerald peepers widened when she realized what she would've done.

My grandmother was not the hugging, touchy-feely type. Any type of affection would raise red flags in anyone's eyes, especially Shadowblood. What she lacked in capacity for warmth and cuddles, she made up for with lots of cash. Nobody would ever see me complaining.

Far be it for me to deny her the urge to buy my love.

"Hazel was hurt?" Ace piped in, and me and Danika looked at each other.

"Did you see the building?" I rushed out before he said anything else. "Half of it dropped on me and Shadowblood." With a strained laugh, I waved off the horror on the beta's face. "I was lucky, and Shadowblood recovered very nicely too. Look at him. He's like a spring chicken now."

"I feel like I'm missing something." The beady-eyed weasel darted his gaze over us.

Danika raised to her full height so she could stare down her nose at him. Momentarily, Shadowblood's shoulders hunched, and he visibly gulped when she slammed the weight of her glare on him. My lips rolled inward to stop the laughter threatening to spill from me.

River had no such issues since he was smirking at the High Priest openly.

"And what might you be missing, Mr. Shadowblood?" My grandmother was one scary-ass witch when someone rubbed her wrong. I almost felt sorry for the dumbass, but then I remembered the shadow tendrils and pushed the pity away, internally cheering for her to fry the pinched expression on his face.

"She's hiding something." One accusing finger wiggled at me. I glared at the priest. "Always causing trouble, and not just for the coven but you as well. I have no doubt all those videos circulating were her doing, just so she could get attention. We stopped them, but people remember things like that."

"Isn't it past your bedtime, pops?" Pointedly, I looked at

the distorted clock on Danika's wall. "We don't want you to have an aneurysm or anything else, goddess forbid."

I bought the time piece for her one year for Summer Solstice, and until a week ago, I'd always wondered why she displayed it when I knew without doubt that she thought it was hideous. Instead of a round face, it looked like the circle had started melting but froze half way through the process, leaving it distorted. The arrows pointing at the roman numerals were skeleton hands with the forefinger outstretched.

At thirteen, I thought it was extremely cool, but later I agreed with her assessment. Yet, it still adorned her wall where everyone could see it.

Shadowblood stuttered in outrage, no doubt ready to throw some nasty reply my way, but the door opened and all of us turned to see who the newcomer was. Sissily's face popped in, and my heart stopped beating for a second. My friend's face was gaunt, and her blue eyes appeared dull and too large for her face. Whatever she'd wanted to say was forgotten the moment she saw me there.

I believe it became obvious to everyone present why I was inside the coven building.

"Sissily ..." My croak was pathetic.

"I'm so sorry, Hazel." We spoke at the same time as she rushed toward me.

My friend wrapped her arms around me, almost toppling us and the torture chair over when she threw herself at me. My chest felt tight when I saw how thin she was, and the signs of exhaustion were clear in the black circles underneath her eyes. Before I could say anything, Sissily pushed back far enough to turn and face Danika, but her hands clutched my arms. The contact made it easier for me to breathe. She didn't hate me, and that was all that mattered to me ... at least until she told us why she had come.

"We have a problem." Everyone stiffened at her angry tone. "Two blocks around the coven, the streets are being cleared out. So far, no sightings within range of the coven, but I'm pretty sure it's demons, with a possible vampire or two."

"How many, do we have present in the building that we can use?" Danika rounded her desk, transforming into a drill Sergeant in a blink of an eye.

"I'm calling Alex." Ace had his phone pressed on the side of his head already.

"A dozen or so fully trained witches, and as many trainees who can hold their own if it comes to a fight," Sissily fired back. "Not counting the three of you." She pointed at my grandmother, River, and the High Priest. "Or the wolf and Hazel."

"Absolutely not." Danika's hand sliced the air with finality. "You." She pointed at Ace, and the beta snapped to attention like a soldier, forgetting his phone. "We will run interference, and you will take my granddaughter back where I left her before you snuck her out." Even in a crisis, she was careful not to say anything in front of Shadowblood.

Did she know that the pack was being attacked multiple times a day? The reason for all the secrecy nagged at me, but I couldn't ask, per se. Plus, I had to pick my battles when she was all barking orders and not caring about opinions.

"I'm already here." Jumping to my feet, I protested defiantly. "I can help."

My gaze was on my friend when I said it because I wanted to judge her reaction. I expected a flinch, or her face blanching like it did that day in the cornfield, maybe even for her to take a step back. Instead, she straightened next to me and pressed her shoulder to mine in our usual united front when faced with Danika's disapproving glare.

"I'll take all three of them with me." River stepped up and locked eyes with my grandmother.

Some silent conversation passed between them that none of us were privy to, and after a long moment, Danika creeped the hell out of me when, for the first time, she relented at a staring match. With an unreadable expression, she nodded once sharply, and without a word stormed out of her office.

Shadowblood was torn between following her or staying behind, but a second later, he darted after my grandmother, his feet shuffling like nuts so he could catch up to her.

"If you are planning on handing us over, I'm warning you, I can now ash your ass with a flick of my wrist." I stabbed a finger at Blondie, who arched an eyebrow at me.

I'd forgotten how perfectly handsome River Blackman was.

There could've been hordes of demons pounding on the door, yet I had no willpower to pull my gaze from his melted-chocolate peepers. The top of his hair had grown a little since I'd seen him last, and my fingers twitched with the need to brush the few strands that had fallen over his forehead away. As if reading my mind, he speared his fingers through it, slicking them back as I tracked the tightening of his shirtsleeve around his bicep.

A warning growl snapped me out of my depraved thoughts, and I jerked my gaze to Ace.

"Oh, great. Dick measuring contests," Sissily chirped sarcastically. "I really missed those. Just like old times."

"You're so dumb." Shoving her shoulder, I snickered. Warmth spread through me when my friend returned the grin.

"You can trust River, Hazel." The joy drained from my face at her softly spoken words.

"As much as you can trust a snake, Sissily. Don't let his pretty face fool you, girl." Sissily wanted to argue on Blondie's behalf, though he just eyed me curiously. "He is hiding something, and I can smell it. Danika can trust him all she wants, but let's not forget that she lied to me all of my life, too."

"You sound very bitter, Miss Byrne." As always, I couldn't tell if Blondie was offended or amused by me.

"Can you blame me?" I deadpanned.

"No." With a sigh, River turned toward the door that Danika had left open in her haste to join our coven mates. "I suppose I cannot, but we don't have time for me to change your mind."

"It'll be okay," Sissily mumbled as she guided me to follow Blondie, Ace silently taking the rear. "Let's kick some demon ass now, because we have a lot to talk about later."

I nodded at my friend and sped up until I passed River. Not because I was in any hurry to deal with hellspawn. I just didn't want the temptation of checking out his ass. I was classy like that.

Our arms brushed when I went by, and he turned his face my way.

"You still think I'm pretty." His suggestive but low tone was meant for my ears only, and it sent my heart galloping into overtime.

Demons.

I needed to kill demons before I did something stupid like rush back and kiss the daylights out of the infuriating man.

There was definitely something wrong with me.

Chapter Six

"Just an FYI, I'm not very good at playing defense."

My announcement was met with snorting and chuckles from all three of them.

"I can't see what's so funny about what I said."

"It's been eight days, Miss. Byrne. We haven't forgotten you in that time." River, ever the helpful one, decided to enlighten me. "We know you too well to think there is anything but teeth and claws for anyone other than Sissily."

The woman in question ducked her head guiltily, but I tugged the arm she had looped around mine and pulled her closer. "Damn straight. You better remember that, Blackman, before you lose an eye."

"Don't listen to him, girl. He's trying to prey on our guilt and insecurities to further his agenda," I mumbled to my friend from the corner of my mouth, purposely loud enough for River to hear. "He can smell it, like a piranha, and he'll chomp on a limb when we least expect it."

My smack-talk had the desired effect, and Sissily smiled warily at me. She had a good point when she said we had a lot to talk about, but we had to deal with whoever was attacking the coven first. Which brought me to another question.

"You think they were scouting the coven in case I showed up?" My question was aimed at Ace, and a deep line formed between his heavy brows. "Or they followed us from pack lands to the city?"

Clustered, we moved as fast as we could without making a run for it toward the part of the coven building that had been demolished when I made my magical debut in a blaze of destruction-filled glory. Having the hallways empty at night was unheard of, yet the smooth obsidian, along with the black pillar candles, were the only things present apart from us. Cracks in the walls spread toward what was left of the glass dome, another reminder that I was nothing but a thorn in Danika's side.

"I was careful when we left pack lands," the beta grumbled while daring Blondie to say otherwise with a scowl aimed in his direction. "Two patrols followed us until we reached the highway in case we came across trouble." His piercing gaze swung to me. "There are no guarantees that they didn't, however. I could've alerted them when I called out after you, too."

A frown puckered my forehead at what he said. I had forgotten that he roared my name after I left him waiting in the dressing rooms. At the time, all I'd wanted was to find Sissily so I could apologize for anything she wanted until she didn't hate me anymore, and I hadn't even considered any consequences that might follow because of my actions. Although I was far from the only Hazel in Cleveland, how many shifters from the Greywood pack would be shouting for one while they hid me on their pack lands?

My thoughts were cut off when two witches bounded

down the hallway, wide-eyed and with an urgency that had my heartbeat spiking. Recognizing one of them, I snatched his arm when he neared me, almost dislocating my shoulder in the process. The poor guy blinked at me like he didn't see us blocking his way until that very moment.

"We have to go to the front entrance." Panting, he tugged on his arm so I would free him.

I tightened my hold.

"What's going on out there, Dean?" The fact that I knew his name disturbed him more than whatever was attacking us. Go figure.

"Umm ... Hazel ... you're here," he stammered until his moss-green gaze darted to the rest of my group and zeroed-in on Blondie. "River, thank the goddess. There are three groups of demons gathering to attack. Two are on the side that's still wide open due to the demolished walls, and we couldn't set wards to protect it." His trembling finger pointed in the direction we were going. "One is coming from the other side. They can use your help over there. Josh and I should be enough to hold them back on our end."

Josh, as I now knew him, bobbed his head and raised a thirteen-inch dark wooden wand like a crooked finger in front of him. A wicked smile curled his lips when all of us took a step back, eyeing the magic conductor like it would bite us. Witches had many ways to aim their magic, mostly by using themselves as a conductor for their power. It took a toll on the body, but it was a matter of ego and pride not to use objects like the wand I stared at warily.

Arrogance aside, a witch would pack more of a punch if they used something like Josh intended to use, and proudly at that. By channeling through the wand, he would be able to last longer in a fight since it'd preserve his energy, especially if he charged it before using it. Which the wood obviously was judging by the prickle I felt on my skin.

The pentagram tattoo on my forefinger thrummed in anticipation.

"Put that away, Stormblood," River barked, and Josh sheepishly lowered the wand. "Go, and don't play heroes. If you need help, call someone."

Hearing his last name, I cocked my head to look at the witch better. I knew Sissily had other family members in the coven, but I'd never personally met them. Josh must be one of the cousins she didn't like hanging around. One glance at my best friend confirmed my suspicions.

Sissily did not look impressed.

"Will do." Dean wiggled out of my grasp and tugged poor Josh with him. "May Hecate lend you strength."

"Let's go." Blondie didn't wait to see them go. "If they left protection of the entrance to those two, things are pretty bad on the other side."

"Josh is an arrogant dumbass, but he is not bad with magic." Sissily hiccupped, and I cut her a sharp glance.

She always got a case of the hiccups when she was nervous. That only served as a reminder that she hadn't been nervous the night she saw the full display of my power. My best friend had been terrified of it. Knees buckling, I rushed to keep up with them.

A scream preceded the scene that opened before our eyes.

A dozen witches were spread out along the broken wall, each one casting magic as fast as a human would fire bullets. Wind was blasting the area outside the building, breaking branches from the trees and pelting the gathered demons with them. Ropes of fire streamed from a couple of my covenmates, igniting the limbs of the greenery and setting our attackers on fire. When I neared close enough to see better, I noticed the ground between the demons and the broken wall was a solid block of ice.

Danika stood like a general at the center of it all, her chin jutted out and her fury-filled emerald gaze locked on the schmucks. Her black-as-midnight ponytail lashed behind her head like the tail of an angry cat. Much to my surprise, Shadowblood stood shoulder-to-shoulder with her, shadows sneaking from his hands in thick tendrils that hissed and snapped toward the demons, daring them to move closer.

"You good?" Warmth spread through me when Sissily leaned closer to me.

"Ya." Blowing a sigh through pursed lips, I shrugged off my jacket. "If you cover me, we can end this in less than a minute." Gnawing on my lip, I stared at my pumps because I wasn't ready to see the expression on her face yet. "As long as no one sees me, we should be good."

"I think you should stay back, Hazel," River murmured from behind me. He stood so close it took great effort not to lean into him, so I couldn't give him crap for using my name. Tongue stuck to the roof of my mouth, I swallowed thickly. "Something doesn't feel right about this. Danika can tell too, and that's why she hasn't obliterated them yet."

Ignoring his nearness, I narrowed my eyes on what I could see from the outside world. The block around the building was clear of any humans, but it wasn't what made me pause. It was the absence of any other sound I associated with the city that poked at my brain.

"They warded the area with demonic magic." Now that I knew what to look for, the reddish shimmer of the air in the distance became somewhat visible. "They didn't want anyone to see what's happening here."

I'd seen this type of warding only once, and on a video feed of all things. Two witches, one inside the ward and one outside, who barely survived the attack had combined what they managed to record on their phones, and that video was used to teach us why it was imperative to be cautious when dealing with demons.

A lesson I'd ignored all my life.

"Alex is here," Ace groaned after his phone chimed somewhere behind me. My grip on the broken wall turned rigid enough for the obsidian to bite into my palms. "I'm of half a mind to walk out and take my chances with the demons."

"Don't be stupid." My nervous laugh earned me an arched eyebrow from Sissily, who was pressed on the wall next to me. "I'll tell him it was all me. Trust me, he won't think anything less of you. I'm very persistent, and your alpha knows that better than anyone else. His hair is grey thanks to my nagging the last nine days."

Why, yes, I had tried to convince him to let me visit the coven that very morning, but he'd kicked me out of his office with the promise of burpees if I didn't remove myself from his sight. It had worked like a charm, but only because Ace had already promised to sneak me out.

The beta groaned as if in pain, but River snickered hyena-style.

My elbow found Blondie's hard abdominal muscles.

"I can't just stand here." Sissily's head jerked in agreement with me. "I don't know what Danika is doing, but whatever it is, it won't hold them back for long."

No sooner had the words left my mouth when a string of colorful curses spilled from Ace's mouth. Anxiety rolled out of the beta in waves that pelted my skin like needles, and I swung around to find his face blanched of all color.

The wolf ignored me and Sissily, which irked me to no end, but when he spoke, I forgot all about his behavior. "An entire kiss of vampires is spreading around the building outside the demonic ward," Ace told River. "Alex just texted that he will try to hold them as long as he can, but he didn't bring enough of our pack to actually fight them off."

"What else?" There was something in his tone that told me there was more.

"Amber is with him."

My blood turned to ice.

Chapter Seven

Lesson 9: *If you are a self-professed asshole, you should stick to it. Caring about people will get you killed.*

"If you don't get out of my way, Blackman, Hecate help me, I will mess your pretty face up." My threat was met with a broad, infuriating grin by said pretty face.

"I'm with you on that one." Sissily glowered at River, who was blocking our way.

"I understand that both of you are worried about Amber, but let me remind you that she is not a helpless female but a shifter. An alpha female, despite her smiles and baked pies," Blondie drawled as if we were dumb and overreacting.

Even if we were both of those things, I needed him out of my way.

Swirling my arm in an overly dramatic fashion like the hostess on a prize-winning TV show, I encompassed the battle behind the broken obsidian wall we used as a shield. Knowing that the sweet woman was out there with vampires and demons circling around her, regardless of her mate being there, made the creature that was my magic pulse under my skin. If I didn't lay eyes on her to assure myself she was okay, I had a niggling feeling I was about to go boom for the second time inside my coven.

"This is not a drill. I repeat, this is not a drill." Mockery didn't work any better than threats did on River. "Let me pass, Blackman."

At least Ace left to rush to his alpha's aid. We only had one arrogant jerk to deal with.

"No." With a sigh, he shook his head at me. "Danika will string us both up using our intestines if I let you out of my sight."

Sissily and I looked at each other, a silent conversation perfected after years of me getting my best friend into all sorts of trouble passing between us. River narrowed his chocolate peepers at us just as Sissily gave me a sharp nod. My heart jumped in joy.

Her hand slashed the air right at Blondie's chest level, and a gust of wind smacked him hard enough to lift his feet off the ground. River was so caught off guard that he wind-milled his arms, but there was no escape for him. My grin hurt my cheeks as I watched him flail. Sissily followed that with another wave of air magic, bouncing him as if he was a fallen leaf on the wind and sending him smacking into a closed door almost a yard away from us.

I snatched her arm and yanked her down the hallway toward the front entrance and as far away from River as we could get. My pumps beat a fast rhythm over the smooth, hard floor, Sissily's flats smacking a duller thump alongside it. Elation filled me. Just like old times, the two of us were bolting down the coven halls hoping to avoid my grandmother. She must've been thinking the same thing because she giggled and squeezed my hand.

"He's going to be pissed." I panted, not daring to slow just yet.

"I say he will rip us a new asshole, but yeah. Let's go with yours. It makes me feel better." Chortling with glee, Sissily kept pace.

"I still don't understand my magic." Finding it imperative to point that out, I cut a side-eye at her. "I won't use it unless I have to."

"I was an idiot, Hazel. Please do what needs to be done so none of ours get hurt. I swear to Hecate that I'll explain my dumbass behavior later."

After I skidded to a stop and whipped my head around wildly to make sure no one was there, I darted toward the double doors with renewed vigor.

"Okay, but if you run again, I swear, Sissily, I'm going to make an anthill out of you, too." If I expected her to so much as blink at the gruesome reminder of what my magic did to the three shifters in the cornfield, I was left wanting.

My best friend shocked me enough to make me stumble when she bared her teeth at me in a challenge. Laughter burst out of me at seeing that unhinged look on her face. I had a feeling she hadn't slept since I last saw her, though mischief danced in her blue eyes and her magic was as strong as ever.

Grinning like a fool, my hand wrapped around the elaborate golden knob on the door, and I put my back into it to swing it open. Sissily did the same, and both doors parted wide enough for us to walk out shoulder-to-shoulder. A scream lodged in my throat when a third person strolled through with their head held high, although those golden strands were windswept and sticking out in all directions.

"Thank you, ladies," River purred and sauntered out of the coven building like he owned the place, his long legs eating up space fast enough that I had to run to catch up to him.

"He is going to give me a heart attack one of these days." I glared daggers at the back of his head, though my hand was pressed firmly between my boobs to hold my heart where it belonged.

"Yeah, that's another thing we need to talk about," Sissily muttered low enough for my ears only when he hurried after Blondie.

As soon as we were outside, it became clear that not just the conversation with my best friend had to wait, but so did everything else. What used to be three groups of demons—according to Dean and Sissily's cousin Josh—turned out to be triple that number, and most of them were clustered around the tall marble stairs. The air shimmered behind them, and it was red from the demonic magic. My heart turned into a fluttering, stuttering mess that was making a valid effort to kill me where I stood.

White noise thundered in my ears.

"Sissily, take Hazel inside." River faced the horde with the confidence of a celestial being.

One sharp look stopped any insanity that would've made my best friend listen to the arrogant man. My rebuttal died on my tongue when Blackman started unbuttoning his shirt, each flick of a button snappy and precise. Mouth dry, I ogled him like an idiot until the soft fabric was released from his fingers and fluttered to the ground.

A howl pierced the night from outside the ward.

It snapped everything into focus like a rubber band.

"Is he planning to kill them by stripping naked?" I

slurred, slurping back drool that had gathered with each roll of muscle on River's back and arms.

"Looking at you, it might work," Sissily griped, poking my side with her finger. "You having a heart attack?"

"I might be." A flinch followed what I blurted out, and my friend snickered.

"No." Sissily held me back when I tried to join Blondie. "He won't need our help, I promise."

"Are you drunk?" Yanking my arm out of her hold, I took two steps. "Can't you see how many—"

Wings as white as the first fallen snow unfurled from River's back, their span stretching from one side of the marble stairs to the other. They opened with a resounding snap that made the demons closest to him jump back with startled shouts. There were all sorts clustered in wait, but most of them were imps and trolls judging by their body shapes and the colors of their hides. The aggression that permeated the air shifted, and horror drenched every breath I sipped through numb lips.

River ignored us while a too-bright glow surrounded his body, and he grew a couple of inches, not just in height but in breadth too. His blond hair extended down his neck until it reached mid-spine and settled between his wings.

I found it difficult to pick my jaw up off the floor.

From any type of shock I kind of expected to come my way when it came to the intriguing man, him being an angel had never crossed my mind. My brain screeched on that thought, and my head whipped toward Sissily.

"I touched him," was the only dumb thing I could say. "You touched him too."

The sigils under my skin writhed and churned from the turbulent emotions that were doing their best to stop my heart. Yawning maw opened in the pit of my stomach and the unpredictable power, with a mind of its own, perked up, its entire attention centered on the being that had not been seen on the Earth for longer than I'd been alive.

"I touched him." Like a broken record, I swiveled my head from River to Sissily.

Angels, including fallen ones, couldn't make physical contact with the rest of us without killing us. Not just humans, but supernaturals as well. Their powers were too strong and very unpredictable, which was one of the reasons they found Earth lacking and disappeared to wherever they were from. We were the dirt under their shoe, and not significant enough to notice or deal with.

"I think he is a Nephilim," Sissily hissed and yanked hard enough on my arm to pop my shoulder out of its socket. I was dumbfounded enough to brush off anything she said because "angel" was on repeat in my head. "Stop gawking like a fool and move your ass before he sees that we are still here."

My pumps were stuck to the ground with gorilla glue.

I was not going anywhere.

"Hazel Byrne," my friend growled, her tone feral enough to make Alex proud.

Anger bubbled up, joining the excitement my magic felt about seeing a goddess-damn angel in the middle of fucking Cleveland. Screams and roars created a symphony of pain in the air when River descended on the demons, his wings lazily flapping to hold him a few feet off the ground. The monsters that made all of us fearful stumbled over their own feet in their futile attempts to get away from him and the fire burning brighter than any I'd seen from his hands.

"I told you saying my full name never works; it only makes me angry," I told Sissily through clenched teeth, not taking my eyes from Blackman.

Blackman, my ass.

Whatever his name was, it sure as hell did not have a witch bloodline connected to it. The more I thought about it, the angrier I became. Staring at him explained a lot of things, including my inability to think with my brain instead of my vagina around him. When I said he was too pretty to be real, I had no idea how right I'd been. And more importantly, how did Danika manage to snag a favor from one of those was anyone's guess.

Another deal, no doubt.

Maybe my soul was what she'd traded for it.

Seething and glaring daggers at Blondie, I almost missed the demon sneaking around him. At first, I dismissed it as a shadow in my periphery, but a string of fire flew from River's palm, and it illuminated that part of the stairs that was previously shrouded in shadows. Bat-like wings poked above the lanky demon's shoulders, and his bald head turned left and right as it moved swiftly away from the massacre. His razor-sharp teeth were bared in a grimace, and the pointy, too-long-for-his-head ears twitched. A thin tail flicked back and forth as he tried to blend with the darkness and disappear.

"Oh, no you don't." Snarling I darted to intercept him, Sissily hot on my heels.

Chapter Eight

The imp shrieked when I planted myself in its way with my glowing arms, sigils churning, and all. Its round, too-large eyes with no pupils were a pitch-black emptiness bulging out at me, and it jumped back a step. In my peripheral vision, I could still see the reddish shimmer of the demonic ward, which contradicted the hordes need to get away. If I wanted to escape certain death, I would've dropped that shit and hightailed it. Which meant someone was holding them inside.

But to what end?

"You shall die, witch," the demon brayed at me. "All of you shall die."

"The only one kicking the bucket here are you and your buddies, dumbass." Rolling my shoulders, I debated how to provoke the magic inside me and get it to make an appearance.

The book, which had mysteriously decided to mail itself to me, so far had offered no answers, its pages as blank as a newly purchased notebook. While on pack lands,

I'd learned how to keep my emotions under control so the ground didn't rattle like an impending earthquake, but nothing else. I counted on the imminent danger to force it out of me, but that was a no-go. I had a nagging feeling that turning into a magical glow stick would not be enough.

Since I didn't attack it, the demon found his courage and pounced on me.

Sissily's shout was drowned by the imp's shrill bellow of a war cry, and I received a face full of demon breath when it latched onto my face. Sulfur and the smell of something rotten filled my nose, making me gag while the damn thing clawed at my cheeks and shoulders. Retching air since nothing would come out of my stomach, I snatched it by one of the wings and yanked as hard as I could.

Claws dragged down my face when I dislodged a demon the size of a house cat on steroids. Adding insult to injury, its tail flicked hard behind it and slapped me across the nose hard enough for my eyes to water. Rivulets trickled, mixing with blood across my cheeks, and I flung the little jerk to the side as hard as I could. Instead of sailing away from me, it latched onto my arm and its razor-sharp teeth sank into my forearm.

My damn magic bubbled and writhed, but it seemed content to allow me to be used as a chew toy. Less screams bounced from a few yards away, but I was too busy with the stupid demon-turned-octopus to be able to check on River. Sissily darted within the trajectory of my arm, which I shook hard in order to dislodge the imp from it.

"Stop moving," my friend snarled right before she finally managed to snatch the twitching tail of the imp.

"Let him gnaw on your arm, and then I'll tell you to stop moving." A shrill squeal was ripped from my throat when she pulled on the tail, and the demon sank his teeth deeper into my skin.

"Sorry." Sissily jerked her shoulders up to her ears as if she could feel my pain. "Hold still just a second so I can grab its jaw and pry it open." Panting, she refused to let go of its cursed tail. I saw stars. "If I use magic, I might blister your skin or burn your arm, but that would be a worst-case scenario."

"Don't you dare." I pushed through my grinding molars.

"Can't you—" She didn't get to finish the sentence because the little shit slapped her across the mug with a leathery wing. If I was not in so much pain, I would've laughed at her gobsmacked expression.

"Who the fuck thought to send imps to attack a witch coven?" Hissing in fury, she slapped at the demon attached to my arm but missed it by far. Its jaw tore more of my skin and sent blinding pain up to my shoulder.

I fought and hid to stay alive only to die from poison administered by an imp bite. Somewhere in the back of my mind, I registered the lack of sound apart from our trio, but it was there one moment and gone the next. My friend was too focused on the imp as well, or she would've prevented the further embarrassment. I was sure of it. Hammering my fist in its head did absolutely nothing to persuade the demon to release the bite, either.

"Im'ma grab it." Sissily pressed her mouth into a firm line, determination burning in her blue peepers and brightening them with a glow that was not diminished by the dark smudges from lack of sleep. "Just grind your teeth, and they'll heal your arm in the infirmary."

"Like hell they will." Appalled by her lack of compassion, I tried to step away from her but couldn't. She had a death grip on the imp's tail. "Release its tail, and I'll deal with it myself." No amount of staring daggers could discourage Sissily when she was on a mission.

"Stop being a cry baby, Hazel. A Brazilian wax hurts more than this. Don't bite your tongue." That was all the warning she gave me before she reared back with both her hands wrapped around the demon's twitching appendage.

A muffled shriek came from the imp, who kept drooling all over my forearm. Thick ropes of its saliva stretched from my arm toward the ground and mixed with big, fat drops of my blood. Our bickering, which was a normal occurrence with Sissily and me, only made the demon frantic and horrified. So, when the full weight of my friend hung from its tail, the hellspawn panicked and, releasing his jaws from my extremity, he turned them on my chest.

Prickly claws embedded themselves between my ribs, luckily not long enough to cause internal damage. It still hurt like a bitch and made me bellow in alarm, which did absolutely nothing to get the little shit off me. Bulging, pitch black eyes locked on my open mouth like a damn dentist inspecting my perfectly healthy teeth only to make up a bogus story about seeing an invisible cavity so I would line their pockets. My trap closed with a loud snap when I noticed its calculating expression just in time. With my tonsils tucked safely away, the crazy demon went for my Prada bralette top.

Hearing the silk rip hurt more than when the imp gnawed on my muscle and bone. The demon and I both started flailing at the same time, and its tail slipped from Sissily's grip, sending her to the ground. She hit it hard on her ass and grunted, staying down instead of helping me save my poor blouse. Well, more like a bra than an actual blouse, but that was the way of fashion in this day and age.

In my panic, magic blasted out of me in one dark, thick pulse, incinerating the imp but not before I saw its face and the silk hanging like a noodle from its jaw. Ash puffed in a cloud around my face, which I had to wave away before I swallowed since I was gasping in outrage. When the patch of remains from the imp cleared, a face came into view from a couple of feet away.

Smoldering chocolate eyes burned into mine.

"Ummm." Sissily's uncertain tone only infuriated me more.

"You are an angel." My finger stabbed the air at River's face like the last twenty minutes or so never happened.

Without comment to confess or disagree with me, his gaze rolled from head to toe slow enough to burn a trail over my skin. Standing my ground, I glared at the liar, not wanting to give him the satisfaction of looking away. My lower belly, on the other hand and thanks to the heated stare, was trying to learn acrobatics, and my vagina was singing praises for Blondie, damn them both.

"Hazel?" Sissily groaned as if in pain, which turned my name into a question.

"What?" I snapped at my friend, not glancing away from River.

"Your boob is out," Sissily croaked, either trying to hold back laughter or mortified on my behalf, but I'd never know which.

My eyes jerked down, and there it was. My left boob was definitely out in all its glory, completely devoid of the poor silk top that covered it. It hurt when my hand slapped it in an attempt to hide it from Blackman's view, a little too late, of course. At least he could no longer be threatened by my pointy nipple, which was stretching as far as it could to get his attention.

"His face is out, too, but you don't see me complaining." Cool as a cucumber, I waved a hand toward River. My friend's snort mingled with Blondie's dark chuckle, which grated on my nerves. "That little shit ate my Prada shirt. Who does that?"

"Demons?" Sissily snickered as she climbed to her feet. "If you stopped moving, both your boobs would be covered right now." Yet, she tugged the t-shirt she was wearing and handed it over.

"I thought hellspawn liked souls, not silk. Color me surprised." Grumbling under my breath, I accepted the offering but arched an eyebrow at the tank top she had underneath.

"I'm prepared now." Her shoulder twitched in a shrug. "I figured you'd be needing shirts or pants in a snap at any time. I have leggings under my pants now."

We both ignored River, whose eyes were drilling holes into me.

A snort escaped me, though it was muffled from the shirt I was wrestling over my head while still having one hand on my poor boob to protect it from the winged man staring from the side. "What, you think I'll start shitting magic, too? Why on earth would I need pants?"

"I never know with you, Hazel." But she was smiling to soften the bite in her words.

"What happened here, Mr. Blackman?" Danika's voice whipped like a belt hissing in the air.

"River sprouted wings," I told my grandmother, primly like a two-year old at show-and-tell day.

Sissily choked, but I jutted my chin as if daring Blondie to say otherwise.

Chapter Nine

Danika ignored my obnoxious outburst and ushered all of us inside the coven building.

Barked orders, more like it, but I didn't point that out.

We left the marble stairs covered in ash, demon innards, and a small pile of aged bones that belonged to the silk chomping imp. Internally, I hoped I could bring the creep back just to rip him limb from limb for exposing my tit to Blondie, but that only sent heat to crawl up my neck when I remembered the way he stared at me with those smoldering peepers of his.

Thankfully I felt more like myself with Sissily by my side, but something had changed between me and River. I couldn't put my finger on it, but it was there, dangling in my face like a noose and taunting me. I'd like to say it was the revelation of his origin, but when I tried to hold onto that, it felt wrong.

"Where is Shadowblood?" I mused as we lumbered toward my grandmother's office.

"We had a few injured in the skirmish," Danika told us

without turning, like that might mess up her queenly progression. "He is making sure they are taken care of in the infirmary."

"Ah, he is making sure they are scared shitless so they won't make a run for it." Fingers snapping, I bobbed my head. "Got it."

Sissily jabbed me in the ribs.

"Did Alex and Amber get through the wards?" My brain caught up with why I'd rushed to get outside in the first place, before River had grown feathers and hellspawn had munched on my bralette to side track me. "Well?"

"Mr. Greywood will be positioned outside the wards until further notice." My mouth opened to yell at her for not caring about their wellbeing, but she had not finished yet. "I gave him and his team the aid they needed until most of the pack arrived. He insisted on standing as frontline."

"Why is the ward still up when we killed all the demons?" I pondered under my breath but received an answer, nonetheless.

"The ward is not just made by demonic magic." River's baritone spiked a shiver up my spine that had nothing to do with hellspawn. "There is black magic interwoven through it. Not much of it, but it's there."

"Yes, I felt it myself." Danika paused in front of the open door and waited, for the first time in her life, for all of us to hobble inside it before she followed. "Do place the ward so we can speak freely, Mr. Blackman." Trepidation rose like a living thing inside me.

One quick glance at Sissily told me my friend wasn't surprised with the information, and that in itself made me twitchy and irritated. Something must've shown on my face because I felt all their eyes on me as I wrenched the uncomfortable chair and plopped on it with a huff.

"Anything you wish to say, Hazel?" Danika challenged after River was done muttering into all the corners of the room, and the air bubble snapped shut around us.

"There is so much that I don't even know where to start, Grandmother." A headache formed behind my eyes, so I rubbed little circles on my temples, which helped nothing.

But her question was just for show. Danika was not done with me.

"Maybe this will teach you to listen when you are told to do something." Striking emerald eyes stabbed me to my soul.

"I don't follow." Cocking my head as if that would help me understand her better, I blinked at her stern face.

"This wasn't—" Sissily jumped to my defense, as always, but Danika was having none of that.

"It was idiotic to leave the one place where you can be protected. And for what?" Each word was a slap in my face.

"Protected from what, Danika?" Body trembling from rage, I jumped to my feet so I could loom over her for once.

My friend recoiled from my outburst, and even River took a step back, which would've pleased me immensely if I was not losing my mind at the time.

"I need to be protected from myself. Not from demons or I don't know what else." Seething, I paced a tight line in front of her desk. "The moment I lit up like a glow stick and destroyed your pride and joy, instead of tucking me away like some deep, dark secret, you should've stopped and at least told me what was happening to me."

Danika watched me with an unreadable expression on her face.

"But, no," I continued huffing, both my arms flopping in agitation. "Oh, no. Danika Byrne explains herself to no one. Well, guess what, lady?" Rounding on her, I slammed both palms on her desk with a slap loud enough to make Sissily jump. "You can look down your nose at me all you want, but it all ends now. Start talking."

"I deserved that." Melting into her comfy-looking chair, she eyed me shrewdly. "I hope you know it was never my intention to come to this, Hazel."

Wind taken out of my sails, I dropped on the hard chair like a rock. "I don't even know what this is, Danika." With a sigh, I wiggled where I sat and stared at my now-healed forearm. "One day I'm freaking out that I'll be shunned for being a dud, and the next I'm tucked away like a dirty sock with a living creature churning inside me that wants to destroy everything. I need to know what's happening to me." After I swallowed thickly, I raised my tear-filled gaze to hers. "Please."

Sissily crouched next to me and took hold of my hands to stop me from twisting my fingers until they snapped. I felt pathetic for begging to hear the truth, but it all hit me at once, and it was now to the point I felt like I would burst into flames if I didn't get it out. Pride be damned if I died from a heart attack or something from bottling shit up. When overwhelmed, I might act like a bratty, underage idiot, but that was my go-to so I could hide the hurt and inadequacy from the world. Including my flesh and blood.

Especially my flesh and blood.

"Our bloodline was always one of the strongest when it came to magic." Danika's gaze took a faraway look, transporting her to a time and place the rest of us couldn't visit. "I too believed that it was simply a strong bloodline, bred true by good magical pairings through generations, until my mother was on her deathbed. That was when she shared our secret, which is to be protected at all costs." Her piercing gaze flicked between River and Sissily. "If this spreads through our world, death is the best outcome for Hazel. I'd like to believe neither of you want to see that."

Sissily bobbed her head, but my eyes were on River. His expression told me he already knew if not all, at least half of what my grandmother was saying.

"Our magic is different since we are the only family that uses ancestral magic. When we activate our powers, we draw not just from our own but from every Byrne witch from the past, as well as the present." My jaw was unhinged and hung loosely. Ancestral magic was a myth, wasn't it? "And because it's not just witch magic that we have in our veins." Her emerald peepers dared me to say something, but my throat was too tight, and my heartbeat was thrumming in my ears. "Each generation has a soul contract to keep it as powerful as it is. And each first-born girl generations back are conceived with a fallen to assure the continuation of power in our bloodline."

That propelled my ass off the chair, and I shoved Sissily away from me, sending her sprawling on the floor.

"I'm half demon?" Danika winced from my shrill shout.

Chapter Ten

"I'm not a demon." My mouth snapped shut when I heard my own ferocious snarl. Holy shit, I sounded like a demon. A feral one, at that. "No one but another fallen, or an angel, can make physical contact. It's a lie."

The horror rattling my bones settled the more I thought about it. Bending down, I tugged Sissily back up and apologized profusely, and she waved me off. So, I could keep my sanity, I pointedly avoided glancing at Blondie, who was a living contradiction to the lies I was selling myself since he held me in his lap like a baby when I lost my shit in this very office only a week ago.

Lesson 10: *Always ask for a DNA test before you go anywhere near a supernatural being. I had to underline it three times to convey the importance of it.*

"If you would let me finish, Hazel," Danika drawled dryly, dragging me out of my wayward thoughts.

"If it involves more crap about demons, I'd rather you

not finish, Danika, thank you very much." I plonked back on the chair and nervously rubbed my palms on my jeans.

The rasp of my skin over the denim was soothing, so I kept doing it, darting my gaze anywhere in the office so I didn't lock eyes with my grandmother or wing man in the corner. Just the thought of River sent my heart into a frantic hammering. Could I touch him because I had half demon blood in me? I racked my brain to remember if I'd seen Sissily touch him, but for the life of me, I couldn't remember one way or another.

"Your mother broke the tradition." My bones turned to goo, and I melted into the uncomfortable chair like an ice cube left outside in the middle of summer. I wanted to hug the damn torture device because I felt as light as a feather and almost floated away on a nonexistent wing.

Danika, as usual, kicked me in the kidneys the moment I experienced happiness.

"She not only chose to break the tradition, but she fell in love with your father, too." My grandmother's gaze flicked momentarily to River, and all the blood curdled in my veins. "I must admit I was not pleased with her actions and voiced my objections, some may say, harshly."

"You can say it." Hysterical laughter bubbled and spilled out through my numb lips. "You were a bitch. It's okay, we all know you here."

Her lips, which were painted a glossy red like she just applied the lipstick, twitched up at my blabbering.

Regally, Danika inclined her head like a goddess-damn swan. "I was a bitch, yes." No remorse could be seen in her cold, emerald eyes.

"Now we're getting somewhere." My muttering earned me a pinch from Sissily.

If I ended up with yet another bruise, I planned on

kicking her in the ass, if I was still sane by the time my grandmother was done spilling her black soulless guts.

"You cannot pour water into acid and expect it not to violently boil over and splatter everywhere, Hazel." Her ramrod back relaxed in the leather chair. "I might've been harsh but only to protect her, and by circumstance, you as well. I firmly believed she wouldn't be able to conceive, if I'm being brutally honest."

Another calculating look crossed her peepers, but I was anesthetized from being smacked with one shock after another by then. All I could do was blink.

"That is why, when you were born, your tiny body couldn't contain the amount of magic in your blood. I did what I had to do to save one of you, since I couldn't save both." Danika's tongue darted out to wet her lips, a nervous gesture that didn't sit well with me. "I never expected Leviathan to dig around and learn what I was trying to hide by binding your magic."

"Who is my father?" Just saying the word I never thought I'd voice plonked my stomach to the floor so it could splash at my feet. "Is he alive? What is he?"

Acid churned inside me, bubbling in my gut worse than if I'd drank two bottles of tequila and eaten a bag of jalapeños at the same time. Not a good combo, and I was speaking from experience.

"I never met him. Your mother was too smart for her own good." Head cocked to the side, her features softened for a split second. "You remind me of her very much."

The hope that flickered, although unwanted, hurt when it died as suddenly as it appeared. "So, you don't even know what he is. Or what he was, if he is no longer alive?"

"I never said that. I said I never met him." Gaze darting

between mine, she leaned forward, and I forgot how to breathe.

Sissily stepped behind me, and the weight of her hand when it wrapped around my shoulder gave me the strength to inflate my shriveling lungs. It's okay, Hazel. No matter what Danika says, it changes nothing. You'll be fine, you always are. But not even I believed the insistent voice inside my head. I was not fine. I'd never be fine again for the rest of my life judging by the hesitation I could see in Danika.

"Your father was one of the Fae." Silence stretched after my grandmother delivered that nail in my metaphorical coffin. "You can see how that ancient magic mixed with what you had already genetically inherited through your mother could be a problem in a newborn child."

"You never intended to unlock my magic, did you?" It all shifted and rearranged itself inside my head like the pieces of a puzzle, and everything came to me in a whoosh.

For almost a month, Danika had been acting snappy and frustrated, disappearing for hours if not days. All the punishments were not just to keep me out of sight from the covens. It was to buy time for herself, too. As I voiced my suspicions, I could already see the confirmation of my accusation written all over her face. She had the decency to pretend she was ashamed, I'd give her that.

"I did not, no." With a patronizing sigh like I was being difficult, she pierced me with one of her trademark scowls. "You must understand, everything I've done is for your own good, Hazel."

"Are you sure about that?" Because I sure as fuck was not. "Let's stop with the bullshit, mm-kay?" Another thought slapped me like a wet sock across the face. "You also asked River to come and join the coven. Now we know he sprouts wings. Imagine that, huh?" Widening my eyes, I mockingly gaped at her. "Pretty boy is here to do what, exactly? Kill me if I get too out of control?"

Sissily's gasp was drowned by the animalistic growl coming from deep within Blondie's chest. My friend's grip on my shoulder at that point was painful as hell, but it helped keep me grounded so I didn't slap her away.

"Aww, I'm sorry." Titling my face, I fluttered my eyelashes at River's furious glare. "Did I hurt your feelings, pigeon?" A firm press of his mouth was my answer.

"You have every right to be angry, Hazel," my grandmother interjected before Blondie and I started on each other.

I decided I'd deal with him later. "You don't say."

"As I was saying," Danika snapped, forcing me to clench my jaw so I didn't yell at her, "be angry with me all you want. I would do it all again, and I won't apologize for anything. You have magic that none of us have seen until now. You understand that, don't you? It could be destructive, for all we know. If hating me makes things better and helps you cope with the burden your mother bestowed you with, so be it. But make no mistake, Hazel Byrne, I saved your life at the cost of my own child. If you don't control yourself, I will also take it away. Believe me, I don't need Mr. Blackman's help for that."

The expression I'd seen many times but only fleetingly on her, the one I could never decipher, hit me like a brick and left me dazed. Resentment. Danika hated every breath I took because she had to save me instead of her daughter. Indignation spread through me, but I bit the inside of my cheek and held it down. I could argue that I'd never asked for any of it, but I knew it'd make no difference.

Nothing ever did when Danika set her mind on things.

"Did you just threaten me?" Flabbergasted, I searched

my grandmother's face, hoping with everything in me that I was wrong.

"Don't be absurd." My tense shoulders sagged a tad bit too fast. "I'm only telling you the truth, as I promised. I left you in Mr. Greywood's care because I know he can protect you while I search for a way to train you on how to use your powers. Obviously, it was too much to ask for you to do what you are told for once in your life."

"That's where you are wrong. You see, I have no problem doing what I'm told." Anger started warming my chilled insides. "What I have big issues with is being pushed around like some inanimate object with no explanations and half-truths. You get what I'm saying?"

Amber would be proud when I told her that, despite all the bombs Danika had dropped on my head like a pro-baseball player, I had kept a tight leash on my emotional state. Well, as far as the magic was concerned. The ground didn't rattle, and I didn't blast anyone into a decorative pile of bones. For everything else, I was ready to be locked up in a padded room.

"She deserves to know the truth." Sissily's tone, although barely above a whisper, made more impact on Danika than all my raging. My grandmother sucked in a sharp breath. "You know, all these years, I believed that everything you did, the way you treated Hazel ... that it was to make her tough. Because you loved her too much and wanted to protect her from all the harsh, unnecessary words the world would throw her way." Twisting at the waist, I watched a tear trickle down my friend's face, and my chest felt so tight it physically hurt. "But you are just as stupid as me," Sissily spat in disgust.

A jolt rocked my body.

Sissily had never dared say a wrong word to my grandmother, even when she stood up for me. To hear her call Danika stupid, in her face, was something I'd remember for as long as I lived. Or as short. Seeing my grandmother's face was priceless. But Sissily was not done.

"You are afraid," my friend accused, with a trembling finger aimed at Danika as more tears made tracks down her cheeks. "When I saw the power manifest from Hazel, I was angry and felt betrayed." Her glossy blue eyes slowly lowered and landed on my face. "I thought you knew all this time but never trusted me enough to say a word. I'm a dumbass. I know that now, but it's the truth. Even after your grandmother confessed about making a deal with Leviathan to seal your magic, I thought it was just a story the two of you agreed on so no one would know the truth of what really happened."

"I would never—"

"I know, Hazel. I swear I do. I just needed time to get my head out of my ass." She sob-laughed and swiped at her eyes with the back of her hand. "After replaying every second for a week with no sleep, I came to tell Danika that I was coming to pack lands so I could beg you to forgive me. But I found you here, instead. I wanted to apologize. I hate that you thought I was afraid of you."

"No need to apologize, but you owe me one now." My smile wobbled with hers.

"Like I would ever be scared of you, big jerk." She socked me on the back of my head. "Magic or not, I'd still kick your ass."

I had my friend next to me in the middle of a shit storm. One ass kicking was nothing as long as she had my back.

Chapter Eleven

"She's lying."

Head craning to make sure no one was around, I followed Sissily toward the infirmary. After noticing that I'd figured most of it out, if not all, Danika kicked us out with some crap about my wellbeing. Apparently, the imp bite had to be checked before we wasted time discovering all her deceit, although my forearm was already healed. My poor boob was traumatized from being shamelessly exposed, but my skin was as good as new. At this point, I believed that short of someone chopping my head off, I'd be good.

More than good, actually.

"I think so, too," Sissily gibbered, unconcerned if anyone heard us as she stewed in her anger as well. "I feel so dumb, you have no idea. Instead of being a jerk and convincing myself that you didn't tell me the truth, I should've been on her ass to see what she was up to. I want to rip my hair out right now."

"Down, girl. Your poor hair has nothing to do with this." She slapped my hand hard when I tried to pat her head. "I hate to say this, but I kinda wish I was a dud after all the admissions from queen bitch."

"No, you don't." My friend rounded on me so fast I jerked back with a jump and landed in a crouch. "Don't even think about it, Hazel Byrne. You hear me?"

"Whoa. Easy, killer." Both hands raised in surrender, I watched her face redden like a tomato ready to explode. "Not thinking about it. See? My brain is as blank as hearing a flatline in cardiology, so calm down."

In the middle of the spine-chilling hallway was the last place I wanted to be, but I waited while she snorted air through flared nostrils until she finally rained in whatever had disconcerted her. Heartbeat jangling my ribs, I searched her face. Me joking about having no magic had triggered something in my friend that had nothing to do with it. I had to get to the bottom of it in a roundabout way and without losing a limb.

Magic crackled at her fingertips as she clenched and unclenched them.

"Fancy seeing you here," I jibed when she calmed down. "Do you come here often?"

With a jerk of her head and a flat expression, Sissily ordered me to continue walking. She didn't even crack a smile at my joke. That unnerved me more than anything. I dawdled a step behind her, tracking her jerky movements, which only piled more dread inside my belly. The feeling worsened when she took a different turn and stomped in the direction of the ritual chambers instead of the infirmary. After scrubbing all the damn wax for weeks on end, neither of us wanted to see the cursed rooms in the next lifetime, and I would've rather faced Shadowblood than be inside those.

"I don't think River knew all of it." My hand froze on

the doorknob as I was closing the door when she announced it under her breath.

"Knew what, exactly?" Turning to face her where she paced in front of the slab used as an altar, I leaned back so the closed door supported my weight. My arms folded across my chest in a defensive stance I hated but couldn't stop. "That he will be my executioner, or that he sprouted wings. Because let me tell you, if I had that many feathers up my ass, I'd know it, you can bet your sweet pea on that."

"I'm not talking about his wings, girl. That's the least of our problems." Hand flopping in front of her, she grimaced and dismissed the one thing that made me livid in a very un-Sissily-like manner.

"You may not, but I want to talk about them very much, mm-kay? Because what in the actual fuck, Sissily? Did anyone think for a second that maybe I needed to know what he was before he stepped within arm's reach?" Voice raising, I narrowed my eyes at her. "You knew and didn't tell me. Wanna talk about betrayal?"

"You really are dense if you think I'd hide something like that from you." My arched eyebrow reddened her face again, but she explained herself dutifully. "Day before yesterday, I needed to expel some magic before I pulled a Hazel and blew up my house." Her blue peepers glittered as I glowered at her through barely open lids. "He was in the training facility that morning when no one else but humans were around. Danika hired some human company to clean up the mess and start rebuilding because she doesn't trust any supernaturals around the coven at the moment. Well, I walked in when River thought he was free to stretch those puppies out. You can imagine my reaction when I walked in on a room full of wings."

"Im'ma pull a raccoon with rabies on pretty boy, watch

me. Jump with claws outstretched and scratch his eyes out. I want to pop those peepers like grapes, shove them in a jar, and let him carry them everywhere he goes," I seethed, grinding my molars.

"You know what's sad? I can actually see you doing it." Some of the anger dialed back, and my friend snickered at my animated and gruesome explanation of my plan to mutilate River.

"I can't believe I'm saying this, but I'm looking forward to going back on pack lands." Fatigued and shattered from everything, I wobbled to the side and slid down the wall to hug my knees. "It's been nothing but a shit show for me around Danika and the coven."

"Even around me?" Joining me where I huddled, she slid down and bumped her side on mine before plopping her head on my shoulder. "We'll figure it out, girl. It will take time, but we will."

"What did Blondie do when you walked in on him basically waving a dick around while he thought no one was looking?" Heat spread through me just thinking about wing boy naked, but I stomped hard on it.

Snorting, Sissily wiggled until she was comfortable, going as far as readjusting my limbs to her liking. She twisted me like a damn pretzel, yet I didn't complain. The woman wore extra clothing in case I needed them, so I'd suffer discomfort for her like a champ any day.

"Surprisingly, he didn't freak out." Her chipped nail raked on the seam of my jeans. "I know he didn't sense me until I was inside the training facility, but the second I stepped foot in there, he turned around. I was terrified, as you can imagine, but the first thing that popped into my head was the way he held you after you went kaboom." Her shoulder twitched in a shrug. "I figured I'd hear him out before condemning him for being a mendacious person."

"Oh, there are a lot of lies going on between him and Danika, believe me. Both can say whatever they want. I'm refusing to trust a word that comes out of their mouths."

"You would, wouldn't you?"

"What's that supposed to mean?" Irked by the defensiveness in my tone, I still stood my ground. "I'm jaded, Sissily, not an idiot."

"Don't bite. I'm just saying I know that you'll be apprehensive after everything that's happened. I'd be worried if you weren't." Peering at me, she smiled sadly. "I'm pissed that they made you like that, but I'd never blame you for it. As for River ... I honestly don't think he has any malicious plans when it comes to you. He is hiding something, yes. I'm just not sure it has anything to do with you and what happened."

I chose to ignore that comment. "You said Nephilim when I received the mother of all shocks, but I was too preoccupied with the imp to ask more questions afterward."

"That's what he said was the closest comparison to what he is. His father is apparently a witch, a rogue one, mind you, and an old friend of Danika's. His mother was an angel, a minor celestial being that had a blessing from Archangel Raphael to conceive a child. If I understood him correctly, she dropped him off a few days after he was born on his father's doorstep, and they never heard from her again. River agreed to help Danika protect you because she promised him she'd help him find his mother."

"That explains it." My groan was long and sounded way too tortured.

"Explains what?"

"Why he has fire magic and doesn't give two shits about

who knows it. The way he displays it on his cufflinks ... that power comes from his father's bloodline, but he has another punch that will knock anyone's lights out if they test him, thanks to his mother." My head thumped hard on the wall. Knowing everything Sissily shared made it difficult to be angry at Blondie, which was not a good thing by a long shot.

"So, why do you sound like you're about to give birth to a baby dinosaur? What's with the groan?"

"After everything you told me, I have to feel bad for hating him now."

Sissily's giggle was cut short when the door swung open.

Chapter Twelve

My heart lurched so hard it felt like it punched the roof of my mouth, but I had no time to react to anything when a golden shimmer burst out of me and formed a wavering circle around us. Sissily slapped a hand over her mouth so she didn't make a sound but, her blue peepers would give a fly a run for its money. One thing we had going for us was the fact that the door opened to the left, which placed us behind it when it was opened.

"It's empty." A hushed voice spoke from the other side of it. "Hurry up."

Two figures rushed inside, slamming the door shut behind them. When we entered, neither of us bothered with lighting the candles spread all over the place, which left only the dim blue light coming from the black pillar ones to cast shadows around the ritual room. Probably why the two men thought they were the only ones inside. They didn't need more light, either, because they stopped a few feet from where we were frozen and stared at each other silently. A million excuses jumped on my tongue for when they finally noticed us, especially when Shadowblood's face came into view, but they didn't spare us a glance.

We looked at each other in confusion.

The second person was Josh, of all people. I had totally forgotten about Dean and Sissily's cousin until then, and seeing the other witch sent panic clawing at me. They were running toward the front doors when we intercepted them in the hallway, and none of us bothered to see if they were still there. Did they notice River's wings?

"Well? Did you see anything?" Shadowblood's nasal tone scraped on my nerves like nails over a chalkboard.

"They didn't come until much later, so no," Josh drawled haughtily. "You'll excuse me for being preoccupied when over three dozen demons passed through the wards they placed around the building."

"They can't see us," I mouthed to Sissily, and wide-eyed, she bobbed her head in agreement.

"You were hiding, is what you mean," Shadowblood hissed, spittle spraying through his thin lips. "Pathetic waste of magic you are."

"I agreed to help you because those videos, before they had them deleted, were creepy as hell, High Priest. I never agreed to be insulted while doing you a favor." To Josh's credit, he squared his shoulders and glared at the older man.

Now that I knew they couldn't see us, I couldn't stand in the same spot. Whatever my magic was doing kept us hidden, so I planned on taking advantage of that. Petty? Yes, it was. Did I care? Not for one second.

Yanking a still perplexed Sissily alongside me, I tiptoed as close as I dared toward the duo. My friend raked her nails over my arm to stop me, but I smacked her hands away and propelled her forward. I had proof that Shadowblood was recruiting others to spy on me, so that gave me the right to mess with his head as much as I wanted.

"It'd be a shame if your family loses favor with Danika Byrne, don't you think, young Josh?" My teeth ground together when I heard him use my grandmother's name to threaten the guy.

I could bet my new-found magic that Danika would love that when I told her.

Quiet as a mouse, I slinked as close as I could get to the old creep without touching him. There had always been a very distinct scent following the High Priest that reminded me of moth balls and some herb with a heavy earthy smell, but the moment I stood close enough, the sour tang of old blood magic nearly doubled me over. The odor was not present when he'd cornered me while I'd searched for Sissily, but there was no mistaking it now when I was practically breathing down his neck.

Silently gagging, I tapped my nose to signal my friend to sniff him. Sissily recoiled at the idea, but luckily for me, she couldn't argue. Taking hold of the back of her head, I jerked her forward, almost mushing her face in the old man's neck. She struggled for just a moment, but I knew the exact moment the stench filled her nostrils. She turned rigid, and all the blood drained from her face.

All color vanished from Josh's face, too, after Shadowblood threatened him in a not-so-subtle way. I would've felt bad for him if the jerk wasn't trying to spy on me and those around me.

"There is no shame in staying alive. So what if we hid? Did you see the demons? They had soul eaters with them, too. Better to lose favor with Ms. Byrne than end up dead." Josh grew a backbone, although I could see his hands shaking.

After hearing their conversation, I had no warm fuzzies for Sissily's cousin, but I hated bullies more. And that was what Shadowblood was doing. Bullying Josh to do his bidding so he could keep his hands clean. I reared back when the old man raised his hand and pointed his forefinger at Josh's chest. A long, dark tendril sprung to life, and while I couldn't hear the softly murmured incantation under his breath, I knew a curse when I saw one. It uncoiled toward the young witch before he could do anything but gasp.

Acting on instinct, my hand shot out and my palm intercepted the magic an inch from Josh's heart. A bright light burst, blinding all of us when the curse made contact, but it blinked out fast. Colorful spots danced at the corners of my vision, yet I still saw Shadowblood jerkily turn this way and that, searching to see who'd blocked his power. Josh gaped at his chest with an unhinged jaw, and a quick check confirmed that the wavering light was firmly in place.

Smugly, I grinned at the weasel, even though he couldn't see me.

Sissily swayed on her feet, and I caught her before she dived to hug the floor. She wrapped herself around my arm like a baby koala and patted me weakly to let me know she was okay.

"How did you do that?" the High Priest snapped, but it sounded more like "how dare you block my curse when I'm trying to kill you," and my eyebrows hit my hairline. The insolence of the man was astounding.

"You tried to kill me." Josh's tone was threadbare, and I almost didn't hear him.

"How. Did. You. Do. It?" Pushing each word through clenched teeth, he snarled at the younger witch.

"I don't know," Josh yelled when the shock wore off and panic twisted his features. "You tried to kill me. Blond hair just like Sissily's fell over his eyes, and he yanked it back. "What in Hecate's name is wrong with you?"

"Lower your voice …" Shadowblood took a threatening step forward, but I'd had enough. Regardless of what Josh felt, my friend was shaking like a leaf watching her cousin almost die. She might not like any of them much, but they were family.

"Step away from him." My voice rang out loud and clear, and it was much calmer than I expected.

Shadowblood looked like he'd sucked on a dirty sock when the shimmering light faded, and when his beady eyes locked on mine an inch from his face, I almost laughed at his pinched expression. Josh shrieked like a little girl and threw himself back, but I ignored him. Sissily detached herself from me and rushed to help him up where he landed on his ass on the floor.

"How did you get here?" Suspicion made his weaselly eyes dart around the room.

"Through the door, just like you." My magic ignored my need when I faced the demons, but it was a churning ocean in my chest this close to Shadowblood. At least we agreed on one thing.

We both hated the High Priest.

"This is her doing," Shadowblood sneered, his knobbed forefinger pointed at Sissily.

"Don't even think about it." I had his crooked finger in my grasp in an instant and twisted it hard enough to buckle his knees. "Before you gather enough magic to hurt her, I'll feed you your black heart."

"Release me, you stupid girl …"

A high-pitched scream ripped from his throat when I wrenched with everything in me and snapped the bone. An insatiable hunger opened like an abyss inside me, and I could've sworn that I tasted his pain on my tongue. Whispers, faint at first but gaining in volume, filled my thoughts, and I pounced on the old witch. My fists hammered at any opening I could find until he sprawled on the floor. I followed him down, and after I straddled him, I continued pounding on his flesh. Each time his muttered curses flew from his hands while he failed to ward off my attacks, they burst in a flash of light that formed stars blinking at the edges of my vision.

Muffled voices droned somewhere in the background, but they were far away enough it was easy to ignore them. This close to Shadowblood, the stench of the blood magic only fed my fury. The creature inside me recognized something in the sour odor that drove it insane. It wanted the High Priest dead, not just to hurt him.

My body became airborne when I was plucked from Shadowblood.

After flopping around for a moment in my attempts to return to pummeling the old witch, I blinked rapidly in hopes of bringing the present into focus. When I saw the bloody mess in a heap on the floor, I sagged in River's arms. I didn't need to see Blondie to know it was him. My nose and lungs were full of his fresh scent despite the blood dripping from my knuckles and covering my jeans. I'd never admit it to anyone, but I had a feeling wing man was the only one who could've pulled me back from whatever insanity had taken over my head.

"Easy there, Miss Byrne," Blondie murmured in my ear, holding me in the air like I was no heavier than a feather. Speaking of feathers ...

"Put me down, pigeon. You don't want to keep Shadowblood company in the infirmary." Neither River nor Sissily looked impressed by the nickname I gave Blondie.

Tough crowd, these ones.

"Can I trust you not to attack him?" The way he said it, low and too close to my ear, had me shivering in his hold.

A few things became obvious then. Danika stood to the side, ignoring the bloody pile of High Priest I left her in the middle of a ritual room like some cadaverous offering, her calculating gaze locked on me. River was squeezing me to his chest as if someone was trying to take me from him, to be precise. And Sissily was crouched next to a paler-than-a-sheep Josh, who gawked at me like I had a penis dangling from my forehead. With a huff, I sagged in Blondie's hold.

"Well. This is awkward." Slithering out of the vise-like grip, I tugged on my borrowed t-shirt for no reason at all.

"I hope there is an explanation as to why my High Priest is beaten unconscious on the floor?" One of Danika's perfectly styled eyebrows arrowed up.

"He smells," Sissily blurted out, and I shot her a glare.

"He tried to kill Josh after he threatened him," I told my grandmother. "I had to do something. Plus, yeah. He stinks of old blood magic."

"I already said that." My best friend blushed to her follicles and stuck her tongue out at me.

"Mr. Blackman, take my granddaughter and her friends back to my office. I need to see what this is all about." Danika waved a hand at the heap that was Shadowblood.

"I will break your hand if you touch me." Teeth bared at River, I grabbed Sissily and darted out of the ritual room like my ass was on fire.

I'd deal with imps gnawing on me all day as long as Blondie kept his tentacles away from me. What was worse ... it wasn't because I still didn't trust him around me.

I didn't trust myself when it came to River Blackman.

Chapter Thirteen

Hightailing it out of Danika's sight did not mean I was a coward.

I was an adult witch with a shit ton of magic, which made me a literal powerhouse in the supernatural world. Not many could claim they had a price on their head without lifting a finger, thank you very much. One blown up library and half a coven building notwithstanding, since that was an accident. I was strong, independent, had a killer fashion sense, and I was a tough-as-nails badass when it came to anything and everything. Plus, I had a mean right hook.

Okay, fine, I was scared.

I'd seen what my grandmother could do when she found out someone had crossed her or did something behind her back with my own peepers, and let me tell you, it was fucking ugly. I would bet my newly found magic some of the jars I destroyed held organs from some of those individuals. Shit you not, I felt bad for the bloody pulp that was Shadowblood. What I did to the poor schmuck no doubt paled in comparison to what Danika had in store for him.

My skin prickled with thousands of needles from her power, and we were halfway down the hallway when the wave hit me.

"I think she is using a memory spell on him," Sissily whimpered, her dainty feet circling fast enough to make the roadrunner eat its heart out.

"She wants to see what happened." I wheezed, darting glances behind us as if Danika would lower herself to chase us like a dog. "I have a feeling Shadowblood had something to do with the wards outside. That's why no one could take them down. No one thought to use a spell to fight off our own magic."

"She knew it was an inside job," River announced calmly, and I honestly wanted to whack him one. He wasn't even winded, for Hecate's sake, while I was panting like an oversized cow.

"Of course, she did." My flat tone provoked a twitch of one corner of his lips. "Did she read you your rights after she kicked us out?"

"She wasn't happy about what happened outside." Blondie turned his chocolate gaze pointedly toward Josh, who stomped clumsily next to us.

The young witch—around eighteen was my guess—left Sissily to drag him with us without protest. The poor guy seemed so out of it that I knew nothing we said had registered in his head. Me appearing out of thin air had done a number on him, and his near-death experience with the curse from our High Priest hadn't helped.

"I'm not happy about it either, but I don't see you sweating it." Grumbling under my breath, I yanked on Sissily's arm to slow her down. For goddess's sake, I'd pass out before I had a chance to have my ass chewed by Danika. "Slow down, little jerk. No one is chasing us."

Instant karma had always been my number one enemy.

Twisting my ankle awkwardly, I wobbled in my pumps. My knee gave out, and I pitched to the side with a sort of gasp-shriek-shout while choking on empty air. That forced me to bodily tackle River, who was prowling beside me, and I hacked in his face like a damn cat trying to cough out a hairball when he hugged me to stop me from humping the large pillar candles that were lighting our way.

To his credit, Blondie didn't push me away or look at me in disgust for trying to make out with inanimate objects, albeit involuntarily.

"Are you okay?" His deep baritone pebbled my skin, and I bobbed like a bobblehead since I still couldn't talk.

"I might have a cracked rib or a punctured lung, but I'm okay." Slapping Sissily away after I sucked in a much-needed breath so she would stop pounding on my back like she was dusting an old rug, I glared at her. "The punching bags are in the training facility if you need to release pent-up anger issues, girl. Damn, that hurt."

"Sorry, you scared the shit out of me." My best friend shrugged sheepishly and latched back onto a dazed Josh while River chuckled. "After thinking you died in an explosion when you blew up the coven, I freak out even when you cough. Can't help it."

"Right. Let's not damage the merchandise, mm-kay." My asinine comment had the desired effect, and she cracked a smile. "Maybe we should take him to the infirmary." Jutting my chin in her cousin's direction, I ducked my head to peer at the shorter guy. "He doesn't look so good."

River caught my wrist when I flopped my hand in front of Josh's face to see if anyone was home. The kid blinked at me, but no other reaction followed the slow lowering and raising of his eyelids.

"He will be fine, I assure you." Blondie ushered us forward, not giving the poor guy a second glance. "He is in shock. It's normal."

"You'd be in shock too if he actually saw you pulling feathers out of your ass earlier." Feeling the need to give him the same amount of anxiety that drilled my stomach, I smirked at him. "He was outside with Dean when you ... you know." Spreading my arms wide, I flopped around as if impersonating some half-dead bird, and Sissily chortled.

It was official.

A screw was loose in my head.

"They saw nothing of the sort," Blondie assured me without a twitch to his kissable lips. "Both of them were huddled behind the statues inside the front doors."

"They could've peeked. We can't know for sure."

"We do know." River gave me a side-eyed glance. "The other one is still sitting there with his eyes closed."

The assistant's desk in front of Danika's office sat askew with the chair flipped on its side. I raised an eyebrow in question since it was perfectly lined even after the fight with the demons, but Blackman didn't think I deserved an explanation. He did straighten it, however, and tucked the chair neatly under it before waving us inside.

Sissily busied herself with making Josh comfortable because that was who she was. My friend loved taking care of people while I loved pissing them off. My very existence rubbed many of them wrong, so I just added to their expectations. Who was I to destroy their hopes and beliefs?

While she did that, I moved around Danika's office,

running my fingers along the spines of the books and tapping a statue here and there to push it in its perfect place, all the while feeling River's eyes on me. Nervous energy filled me to the brim, so instead of fidgeting, I decided to move in the hopes it'd pass.

It didn't.

"Were you ever going to tell me?" There was no need to ask in detail. We all knew what I was talking about.

"Yes." The simple way he said that made me look at him over my shoulder. Sincerity was clear in his loaded gaze.

"I'm actually finding that hard to believe." He didn't ask for clarification, just tilted his head slightly to the side. Unable to hold eye contact, I faced the shelves as I continued. "My magic was unstable when the shifters attacked us in that field, yet you fought them with witch magic."

"That was only three shifters, Hazel. You alone could've dealt with them without any magic if you were not worried about the two of us." I hated that he made sense. Why I tried so hard to find inconsistencies when it came to River was beyond me.

"I'm still Miss Byrne to you, Blackman." Avoiding his burning gaze, I shuffled to the torture device that was a guest chair in Danika's world, and after turning it to face River, I lowered on it with a groan. "We are not that close, you and I."

"You call me a pigeon." Amusement rang loud in his tone, and because of that, I had to roll my mouth so it didn't curl into a smile. Damn him.

"I call everyone names, Mr. Blackman. Trust me, you're not that special." Sissily snorted at my gibe but coughed to cover it up.

"It's true," my best friend informed Blondie, her voice

croaking while she suppressed the laughter we could clearly see dancing in her blue eyes.

"Firefly," River mused while eyeballing me critically.

"Huh?" My eloquent reply was answered by a painfully slow growing smile on his handsome face.

My heart tripped over itself before galloping hard enough to make my borrowed t-shirt tremble over my skin. An imaginary feather started tickling the back of my throat, and I pressed my thighs closed to calm down my hormonal reaction to him. None of which he missed, judging by the heating of his gaze, which was glued on me.

"You can call me a pigeon." I had a very bad feeling we were no longer talking about birds or insects, and the conversation had headed toward the deep end of the ocean while I had no clue how to swim. "I will call you a firefly. It's only fair." Insufferably and deliberately, his peepers rolled from my face down my neck and chest before they pointedly settled on the bare skin of my arm.

The weakling that I was, I followed their direction to the blinking sigils under my skin that illuminated it in uneven intervals. Just like a firefly, my mind supplied unnecessarily, and something in me shifted emotionally, but I felt it like a physical sensation.

"Aww, that's sweet," Sissily gushed, and I flung my gaze at her like an accusation. In answer, she jutted her chin as if daring me to call her out on it. And just because she loved making fun of me, she grinned as she said, "Say thank you, Hazel."

"You know I'm not a monkey performing tricks, right?" But I watched Blondie from the corner of my eye, and the soft smile that played on his lips almost undid me. "Why are we here again?"

"Because we can't exit the wards." My friend spoke with so much glee I had half a mind to throw something at her.

"Hazel," a familiar voice bellowed my name loud enough to be heard through the closed door, and it freaked the crap out of me.

My ass lifted a foot off the chair when I jumped.

Chapter Fourteen

Amber burst through the door with a frantic look on her ashen face, and the moment her horror-filled gaze landed on mine, she hurled herself at me from a few feet away. The chair tipped and wobbled on its back legs, sending my heart into my throat, but thankfully we didn't go down. My bones did not fare so well, though, because she wrapped herself around me like cellophane, restricting my oxygen intake as if the older woman was a python ready to swallow me whole.

Panicked, I searched the faces of River and Sissily for help.

"Oh, thank goodness you are alive." Amber sobbed into my hair, digging her slightly elongated nails into my back as she fought the need to shift. "I thought the worst when we were blocked by the ward and saw all the demons surging through it."

"I'm sorry." Tears pricked at the back of my eyes as I awkwardly hugged her back. "I didn't mean to worry you, I swear. I'm fine, I promise."

It spoke volumes about what kind of a person Amber was when my own flesh and blood never blinked an eye no matter what happened to me. The fact that her heart was beating so fast it thumped against my own chest made me feel like shit for sneaking out, but in my defense, I never expected her to react that way.

Alex stormed in a moment later, bare chested but with an air of barely restrained fury that made me stiffen in his mate's arms. Sure that he was about to start raging and probably tell me to never return to his land again, I bit on the inside of my cheek to suppress a whimper. For whatever reason, the idea of never going back sounded too horrible to contemplate. I even flinched when he stomped toward me and pathetically shrunk back so I could hide behind Amber.

"I should smack you right now for scaring us like that," the alpha snarled viciously before his tree-trunk arms curled around both Amber and me.

Flabbergasted, all I could do was gape when I ended up with a face full of bare muscles, and a gasp was ripped out of my chest when I felt the proud man trembling. It took a moment to realize I was continuously mumbling apologies while they held me squeezed between them in a vise-like embrace, and my eyes darted to River, who hadn't moved the entire time. What I saw in his gaze was another punch in the gut.

"I thought you'd be angry," I told the couple honestly. "I hoped to be back before you noticed I was gone, but ..." My voice trailed off because they knew what had happened without me reminding them of it.

"You better believe that I'm angry, young lady." Alex released his punishing hold but kept his hand on my upper arm. "But just because I feel like lecturing you right now, that doesn't mean you didn't scare the daylights out of us. I'm sure I'll find a way to punish you for shortening my life, don't you worry."

Smoothing the wild corkscrews of Amber's hair, I peeked through them to see his face. His mismatched eyes burned with suppressed anger, but I could tell not all of it was aimed at me. "I'd understand if you didn't want me to come back." Him wanting me around his family again, was the last thing I'd expected after what I'd done.

"Is that so?" Alex huffed like I was a dumbass. "My mate loves you as much as she loves our young. They, all of them, think you are some superhero who can do no wrong. My beta disobeyed my orders to do your bidding. Of course, you are coming back."

"What about you?" It was out before I could stop it, and my breath froze in my lungs as I waited for his answer. In just a few days, his opinion of me mattered more than what Danika thought.

"I never turn my back on pack, Hazel. You are not a shifter, but you are pack. Nothing will change that, not even your grandmother's ploys." The truth of his words shone brightly in his mismatched gaze, and hot tears rolled down my cheeks.

"Thank you." My choked gratitude softened the harsh lines on his face. "How are you here? The ward?"

"Danika took it down," Alex informed me as he finally noticed River and turned to offer his hand in greeting. "As soon as we could go through, we rushed to find you so we could see for ourselves that you were unharmed."

"Where is she?" Free of the wild mess that was Amber's hair, I craned my neck to look through the opened door. The older woman's scent of vanilla and freshly baked pastry lingered in my nose, although she had moved to join her mate.

"She came to meet us soon after we arrived and helped hold the vampires back until the rest of the pack arrived. After that? We don't know." It was Amber who answered, and Alex tucked her under his arm. "There was no one in the hallway either when we rushed to find you. I followed your scent to the office."

"You just said she took the wards down." My forehead puckered in confusion, but understanding dawned when the alpha tapped his nose. Of course, he could smell Danika's magic with his heightened senses, so he didn't need to see her.

"How bad is it out there?" River spoke at last, his tone conversational but his body language anything but. His attention was divided between the couple and Sissily, who darted to stand beside me.

"They brought an entire kiss, fledglings and all," the alpha spat in disgust. "There is no honor in killing newly made vampires, despite their penchant for bloodlust. They act on instinct, and whoever gathered them hoped they would be able to breach the ward. If we didn't arrive when we did, this would've been a massacre."

What he said nagged at me. "Unless they followed me through the stores, which took a couple of hours, there is no way I was the reason for the attack. They couldn't organize themselves that fast for this level of attack."

When the pity on the shifter's faces hit me, bile burned its way up my gullet.

"We found the team Ace left behind when he whisked you out of pack lands." Rage pulsed out in a wave from Alex. "All of them were killed and left for me to find. Whoever is behind this, they had enough time to prepare themselves because they knew you'd be coming here." His mismatched gaze flicked to Sissily, who stood behind my chair.

"This is not on Hazel." My best friend spoke in a low, level tone. "If I had her back like I should've instead of acting like I didn't know what kind of person she was, none of this would've happened. She sneaked out to come see me. I should've stayed with her."

"The blame for all of it is on whoever is behind the attacks." Amber's vehemence surprised me. "Not on you or Hazel. No one has the right to play with people's lives, and they will pay for it sooner or later."

"My mate speaks the truth." Alex had his gaze locked on River. "Did you ...Was I mistaken ..." The alpha fumbled for words as a line formed in the middle of his forehead. All of us could tell he was not used to picking words when he wanted to ask anything.

"They know, and yes I did." Blondie tucked a hand in the pocket of his slacks nonchalantly. "There were too many demons to fight off with just magic, plus a handful of soul eaters. I had to use everything at my disposal, or they would've entered the coven and had everyone cornered."

A memory bloomed in my mind's eye from a week or so ago when all of us were in the alpha's office.

Seeing Danika rub a hand down her face was like finding a unicorn. "I asked Mr. Blackman to join the coven personally. He agreed to join me so we could protect you better, Hazel."

"I had no coven until I answered your grandmother's request." River had a quirk at the corners of his full lips that rubbed me wrong. Like he knew something I didn't, and I was too dumb to figure it out. "I assure you, I report to no one but myself, and her."

"Are yours ever going to join this clusterfuck they left us to deal with?" Alex addressed River, but Blondie just shrugged without

comment. That earned him a disapproving shake of a head from the alpha.

That last part made a lot of sense now unlike at the time. "You knew." I stared at Alex. "From day one you knew what River was." It sounded like an accusation because it was.

"I paid the alpha a visit the moment I stepped foot in his town." It was River who answered. "Your grandmother is powerful beyond measure, but I'd rather not step on toes if I can avoid it." Alex nodded in approval, but I was far from impressed.

Everyone and their mother knew what Blondie was apart from me. That was the main reason I sounded like a squeaky wheel. No one bothered to tell me anything, damn it.

"The coast is clear now, I take it?" Tired to my bone marrow, I sagged in the torture device. "I have about ten minutes left in me, tops, before I curl up wherever I am and fall asleep."

The invisibility bubble—or whatever it was—that my magic created in the ritual room to hide us from Shadowblood and cancel all the curses he flung our way, drained me more than I expected. Ever since I'd lowered into the uncomfortable chair, every second that passed had dragged on me until I barely felt my arms and legs. My eyes were as dry as sandpaper, and it was an ongoing battle to lift my eyelids each time I blinked.

"Clear for now," Alex confirmed. "We better get you out of here before they decide to give it another try."

"I couldn't have said it better myself, Mr. Greywood." Danika scared the shit out of me when she spoke. For the first time, I did not feel her coming.

"Great. See ya. I hope you and Mr. Pigeon here don't

miss me too much." I jumped to my feet. My sarcasm received a firm, unimpressed press of my grandmother's mouth, but Blondie grinned at me.

I was on alert the second I saw that infuriating smile.

"Mr. Greywood, Sissily, and Mr. Blackman will accompany my granddaughter while she is under your protection. I hope you don't mind given the new development." Danika's cold, emerald glare dared me to argue with her before it swung to my friend. "A nurse will be here any moment to take young Josh to the infirmary, Sissily. We will take good care of your cousin."

When I sucked in a breath, Sissily pinched my forearm so hard I yelped and saw stars. My mouth stayed shut, though, because her intentions were very clear to my mashed-potato brain. With a simple nod and no words, Alex scooped Amber up and made an exit. I was right on his heels, wanting to get as far away from Danika as I could, but my shoulder blades itched from a gaze pointed there. One quick glance confirmed that Blondie had his eyes locked on me as he sauntered after us.

"If you know what's good for you, you'll stay away from me, wing man." I found it imperative to tell him that.

"Whatever you want, firefly." With a maddening curl to his lips, he winked.

The jerk winked!

Chapter Fifteen

"Why do I get the feeling that this is becoming a habit?" Alex grumbled, scrutinizing me through his barely opened eyelids the next morning.

A mammoth-sized coffee mug was cradled in his large hand with steam curling over it and "Mine is bigger than yours" written in black print—a gift from Stella, I was sure. His wavy hair was mussed from sleep, and his white t-shirt was inside-out, the thread particularly visible on his broad shoulders. I was not a morning person either, so I understood his grumpiness, especially when the sun was blinding us through the large, open windows of his office.

"Because you secretly like it when I annoy you, but you don't want anyone to know?" Snorting at his scrunched-up face, I raised my own mug and sucked on the black coffee like a baby goat on a tit. "Yum, I think I'll ask for a portable IV with the stuff."

"I hear you, kid." Sipping on his own poison, he hummed his approval. "If this has anything to do with cars, clothing, or the like, I'd advise you to rethink your life choices. I'm tired and preoccupied with things like safety. No time for games right now."

"No." Chuckling at his narrowed, mismatched gaze, I leaned back in the overstuffed chair I sat in. "We were all tired last night, and I needed to process things before I said anything." Buying time by sipping coffee, I watched alertness tighten his features over the rim of my mug. His ebony skin had lost its usual healthy glow, and guilt drilled a hole inside me.

The alpha looked as tired as I felt.

"I want to apologize for being selfish and only thinking of myself yesterday while you are doing more than you should so I can keep breathing. It's not enough, and I'll keep saying it until it feels like it is, okay?" Alex nodded guardedly at my heavy sigh. "Sissily is the only person that has been there for me through thick and thin, and I couldn't sleep in peace until I saw her and assured myself that I didn't lose my best friend. My only friend, I should say."

He mimicked my grimace. "I'd like to think you have more than one friend, Hazel." Leaning forward on his desk, he placed the huge mug between both palms and eyed me much too acutely for my liking. "From experience, I know that when standing in the middle of a storm, it's difficult to see the shelter, even when it is right there in front of your nose. I'm not happy that you are going through this ... let us call it a journey for the lack of a better word, since I don't want to look at it as a negative outcome."

"We can agree to disagree on this," I huffed under my breath but didn't interrupt him further.

"As leaders, we all face trying times when we must make difficult choices that may or may not make sense to anyone else. I, by no means, make any excuses for what your grandmother did, but I would be lying if I said I didn't understand it. Some situations require a sacrifice, and I think this was such an occurrence. If you look around you, you'll see that you are better off because of it."

"How do you figure that?" Incredulity rang loud and clear in my tone, but I didn't dial it back.

"Do you remember what I said last night when you asked me if I wanted you back here?" One green and one blue eye with a soft glow searched my face with laser focus. It was unnerving.

"I'm pack." My throat was tight, but I pushed the words out somehow.

"The last person who wasn't a shifter but was considered pack came three hundred years ago." He let that linger for a while so the meaning could fully settle. "Danika's meddling had nothing to do with that. That was all you. So, I'd say you have more than one friend."

"Thank you, and I know that. Well, I know that now because it takes me time to deal with my trust issues," I told him sincerely. "But that's not what I meant with what I said. I just feel like an ass for causing so many problems because I couldn't do what I was told." Danika's words were riding my ass hard ever since she said them.

"I do hope you know, Hazel. We generally don't welcome outsiders into our fold if we don't trust them with our lives. With the lives of our young." Satisfied, he went back to sipping his coffee.

My sweaty hands made my mug slippery, so I placed it gently on his desk and folded them in my lap where he couldn't see them trembling. His last words spiked my anxiety, but I had to be honest with him for my own sanity.

There may not be redemption for my soul, but that didn't mean I had to pile more sins on it.

"I had the opportunity to corner Danika for some answers." Fleetingly, my gaze dropped to the blinking sigils under my skin, the ones the alpha couldn't see from the glamour. "She explained why our magic was different"— The next part got stuck in my throat, but I forced it out— "and why I'm different."

"Why do you look like you are going to be sick? This is a good thing, no?" Alex sat the huge mug on the desk with a harsh thump and raised it from his chair as if he was ready to jump and catch me if I toppled over. "Is this something to do with the symbols on your skin?"

"What?" I gaped at him dumbly as his forehead puckered in confusion. "You can see them?" How was this possible? Apart from Sissily, River, and Danika, nobody else should've been able to see them.

But Alex was nodding cautiously. "Judging by your expression, I shouldn't be seeing them?"

"Glamour was placed over them when the book unlocked my magic." The deeper the line between his eyebrows grew, the more panic clawed at me.

"They appeared the evening of the pack gathering two nights ago. We knew you would eventually tell us what it meant and didn't want to make you uncomfortable."

"We?"

"Amber and me." Alex cocked his head in a very animal-like manner, his mismatched gaze now curiously expecting my arms.

"I wonder what that means." Thinking back, I had a feeling the glamour held since Shadowblood didn't pull out pitchforks and such, but if the alpha couple could see them then ...

Then what? I had no idea, and I was getting sidetracked.

"You mentioned trust, Alex." Steeling my spine, I straightened in the comfy chair. "I'd like to return the favour because I believe you have every right to know the truth, despite what Danika thinks."

The alpha's stillness was unnatural.

Predatory.

"The strength of the magic in the Byrne bloodline apparently comes from generations of deals between my ancestors and some of the fallen. I don't think there are soul contracts involved, or Danika couldn't make one with Leviathan when I was born ... I think. That last part is speculation, so don't take my word for it." My teeth rasped over my lower lip. "Add that to our inherited ancestral magic and you have Danika—a powerhouse on two legs with no one capable of standing against her apart from a celestial being."

Alex whistled low, his gaze as wide as I'd ever seen it. "No wonder she wanted you hidden from magic as long as she could."

"That's not why she turned me into a dud." It would've been comical to see his eyebrows climb as high as they did, but there was no humour left in me. "Apparently, my mother flipped Danika off and fell in love with my father. That's what complicated things, and baby Hazel couldn't contain the magic, so it had to be sealed. According to Danika"—I took a deep breath and exhaled with a loud huff— "he was, or is, a Fae."

Alex barked out a surprised laugh that sounded like it was more out of shock than anything else. "Now, that makes perfect sense." Shaking his head, he stabbed his fingers through his hair in bewilderment. "I should've guessed that some Fae magic was involved."

"You're not upset?" The Fae were nobody's favourite. They were cunning, selfish, and cruel beyond belief when something stood between them and what they felt entitled to. Or so I'd heard. I'd never met one.

"With you? No." Alex kept shaking his head, making the waves of his hair dance on top of it. "Fae magic is closest to nature, so it's raw and wild. Unpredictable and instinctual. Just like our wolves. No wonder you felt like a kindred spirit from the start and we accepted you as pack. Although we are generationally removed for many centuries, wolf shifters are descendants from wargs, which are Fae."

"I didn't know." It was my turn to be gobsmacked.

"This was extremely helpful." Excitement shone in his mismatched gaze, and for the first time since I walked into his office that morning, he genuinely smiled. "Nature is chaotic and volatile, but that is something I do understand —unlike witch magic. We know what we are dealing with now, so it'll be easier to help you learn how to control it."

"Really?" His enthusiasm was addictive, and hope bloomed in my chest. "But the book is still blank, the useless thing. We have no idea where to start."

"Amber showed you how to control your emotions already. We start from the beginning." Gulping the entire contents in his mammoth mug, he plonked it down and stood. "Practice between us is long overdue, Hazel. I hope you are ready."

The feral baring of teeth he gave me looked ecstatic, but it did not promise fun times for me.

At all.

"You should grab another coffee maybe? You did say

you were tired." I rushed to get my dumb ass out of training with the alpha. "Your shirt is inside out, too. Go change it."

Alex kept eye contact as he ripped the t-shirt over his head and tossed it in my face. It smacked me on the nose, and I scrambled to catch it as he prowled out of the office.

"Let's see what you've got, witch." The alpha's dark chuckle sent a chill down my spine.

Chapter Sixteen

"This is not funny." My grumbling was not doing me any favors.

Alex refused to allow me to hide inside the separate building the pack had specifically designed for training. Instead, he waited with the SUV running until I joined him, then drove us to an open patch of land surrounded by a dense forest in the middle of nowhere. No amount of dragging ass helped when I followed him, and I even ground my teeth at the extra pep in his step.

"It's not meant to be," the alpha pointed out as he circled me.

"I'm not even dressed for training." Counting on his dislike when I spoke about designer clothing, I hurried to make my argument. "At the rate I'm going, I'll be broke by the end of the week if I keep messing up all my outfits, Alex. Do you know how much these pants and blouse cost? Do you?"

"Oh, in that case." The stalking stopped, and he straightened. I breathed a sigh of relief. "By all means, let's go back so we can give the demons, the vampires, and the Blackwood pack a call to make sure they let you know when they are planning on attacking you. We don't want you wearing something you are not comfortable fighting in. They should know that if your outfit is expensive, it's a no-go."

I glared, unimpressed. "You are hilarious."

"I know."

That was all the warning I got.

In a pulse of magic, he exploded with a ripple in the air, and instead of the man, a gigantic gray wolf bared his elongated canines at me. With a yelp, I jumped back, and I could've sworn the animal smirked at me. Easily at seven feet tall if he stood on his hind legs, Alex in his animal form was roughly two hundred and fifty pounds of muscle and bigger than any natural wolf could ever be. Shaggy, coarse fur rustled when he shook himself, and my heart skipped a beat the moment his massive head lowered, and his ears pinned to the back of his skull.

"Umm, easy now, big guy, mm-kay," I blabbered, nervous as hell. "You said we'd start from the beginning."

With a shrill scream, I threw myself to the side, rolled roughly for a few feet, and scrambled on my knees when he pounced. My arms and palms ended up all scratched up from twigs and sharp rocks that did their best to split my skin, the bastards. His reputation aside, I had no problem physically fighting Alex. My issue was I didn't want to hurt the alpha if the cursed magic decided it would be a fun thing to try and fry us a wolf. I had to look Amber in the eye eventually, and that was news I never wanted to pass my lips for as long as I lived. Shifters might be tough, but demons were stronger, and I had quite a few kills under my belt when I'd still been a dud.

"I'm not going to fight you, Alex." Snorting air through my nose, I hissed at him. "This was not the plan. I could hurt you."

The damn animal chuckled.

"You know what?" Climbing to my feet, I dusted my pants with jerky, irritated swipes of my bloodied hands. "I'm not doing this with you right now. It was a dumb idea."

Squinting when the harsh sun tried to blind me, I stopped in the direction we came from, but I only made it two feet. The wolf tackled me from the side, not holding anything back. The air was knocked out of my lungs with a hard whoosh, but I twisted as we flew sideways and jammed my forearm under his jaw just in time.

My neck cracked along with the back of my head when we hit the unforgiving ground, sticks with their sharp edges ripping into my skin and blouse. All my bones were rattled when his full weight pressed on me, and his snout almost touched my face. His nose was cold as it brushed against mine, but his breath was hot like a furnace. The alpha snarled deep in his chest, and the feral sound pebbled my skin.

All that time I was focused on not freaking out so I could hold back the unpredictable magic from hurting him. Contrary to my wishes, the sigils pulsed and blinked in a frantic tempo, sending short bursts of golden glows around us. The wolf kept snapping his deadly jaws at my face—so not helping matters—and grinding my teeth, I tucked my knees under his belly. With one solid push, I kicked him off me hard enough to make him whine when he hit the trunk of a tree.

"You're such a jerk." Seething, I clenched my molars until a sharp pain zinged through my skull. "Are you trying to die? Is that it?"

"I have a solution." A smooth baritone reached us from between the trees, and River stepped out looking so out of place in his dress pants, loafers, and button-down shirt that it was ridiculous.

He was hot as hell, but ridiculous, nonetheless.

"Look what the cat dragged in," I drawled, picking twigs and leaves out of my hair as I stood up. "Did you walk or fly here?"

Lips twitching, he leisurely strolled until he was a foot in front of me, his melted chocolate peepers glittered with golden flecks that reflected the bright sun. "Drove actually."

Alex growled deep in his chest, and I agreed with him. The whole thing was a very dumb idea, and we didn't need an audience for it, either. Which I not so politely explained to Blondie.

"As I said, I can help so the two of you can practise without any harm," River addressed the alpha, ignoring the death stares I was shooting at his pretty face. A slow, cocky-as-fuck smile curled his lips as if he'd heard my thoughts. "I can place a protection against magic around you. That way if she does burst without control, no one will be hurt."

"You can do that?" Eyeing him dubiously, my hands stilled through my hair.

"A perk." River shrugged coolly.

Alex and I glanced at each other, and before I could start drilling Blondie for more details, the grey wolf padded toward him. His mismatched gaze was narrowed in suspicion, yet there was no hesitation in the alpha. It spoke of trust that I personally didn't think River deserved, but that was only because he'd lied to me. By omission, I'd give him that, but still a lie in my book.

I was tired of untruths and secrets.

River reached a hand toward the wolf's head but didn't

touch him. Fingers splayed wide, he hummed something inaudible under his breath, and warmth spread through the air with a soft white light. It circled the alpha, who stood stiff as a board, and a moment later started dissipating. Blondie's hand curled into a fist before he lowered it to his side.

"This explains why you jumped a few dozen demons without blinking an eye," I muttered glumly. "You can shield yourself from magic."

I went rigid when he reached for me, but he only plucked a leaf I missed from my hair and twirled it between his fingers. His scent filled my lungs, awakening feathers that tickled the back of my throat, and I took a wide step away from him. An unreadable expression crossed his gaze, which was locked on me, but Alex was shaking off whatever sensation he was suffering so I focused on him.

"You can go now." Of course, wing man ignored my demand and settled to watch with his back pressed to a tree and his arms folded across his chest.

A branch snapping told me I was tracking River like an idiot when Alex was ready to attack. The difference was, I didn't have to hold back anymore. A wicked grin stretching my cheeks, I found the alpha's position from the corner of my eye, and this time, I jumped at him. It took him by surprise, and he tried to evade me with no luck. With all my weight, I landed on top of him and wrapped my arms just under his front legs. The momentum propelled me forward, and I flipped the wolf who was twice my weight until I had him in a chokehold.

My sigils went berserk, pulsing and blinking, just as the magic swirled in my chest. Alex snarled viciously, jerking his body out of my grasp and leaving me fistfuls of fur when he shook me off him. His upper lip curled above razor-sharp teeth, and he snapped his jaws in a warning, unhappy that I had the upper hand. My legs kicked up, and I flipped myself to standing, still grinning like a fool. Dark shadows danced around me with blood-red streaks spider webbing through them.

The wolf cocked his head in interest, studying the power shimmering around me while I wondered why it'd made an appearance when it was nowhere to be found the night before when I'd faced hordes of demons. Testing boundaries, I flicked my wrist in a spot in front of the shifter's front legs. Power shot from my fingertips, spearing the earth hard enough for chunks of grass and soil to fly in the air, leaving a hole a few inches deep. Alex wrenched himself aside just in time with a yelp.

I saw the movement coming from my left just in time to bend my back as a fist passed a hairsbreadth from the tip of my nose. River decided to join the fun instead of playing a bystander, and that was fine with me. I used the motion to drop down and swirl, kicking my foot out and swiping his legs from under him. Instead of dropping like a rock, Blondie did a backflip, landing on both feet like a cat.

Both continued attacking in sync, forcing me to stay on defence for some time until I'd had enough of dodging kicks, fists, and snapping jaws. I lost myself in the movements of my body, the familiarity of it calming the turbulence in my mind. My magic followed, zapping from my hands when I needed them to pull back, an instinctual precision assuring that I never aimed it directly at them. Just close enough to keep them on their toes. It felt like forever when they moved far enough away, and we all panted, staring at each other.

One glance around made me cringe at the devastation we'd caused in the clearing. While in the moment, I didn't care where my magic struck as long as I stayed on my feet and didn't lose the fight. Seeing the holes in the ground and the broken trees littering the area like corpses didn't make me warm and fuzzy inside as I gasped for air.

"I think I needed that." Wiping the sweat from my face with a forearm, I had to admit it felt good to finally use my power with some control. "Thank you, River."

Blondie blinked like he'd seen me for the first time. I guessed my gratitude shocked him, go figure.

"For what?" His smouldering gaze rose goosebumps over my already-overheated skin. Alex shifted and disappeared through the trees in search of clothing, thank the goddess.

"For placing the shield against my magic around both of you. I didn't have to worry that I'd hurt you, so it was easier to pay attention to controlling it," I told him honestly.

"There is no shield against magic, firefly." I blinked dumbly at him, not understanding. "Not even angels can place a protection against it. You can't kill a celestial, maybe, but you can definitely hurt them."

"But ... but I saw you ..." I stuttered, all the blood draining from my face.

"He just made sure you didn't hold back, Hazel." Alex came back, tugging a t-shirt with the right side out this time over his head. "You honour me by giving me your trust. I think it's time you start trusting yourself."

"River." The warning in my tone only curled his infuriatingly kissable mouth.

Chapter Seventeen

"I'm going to pluck his feathers one by one and feed them to him." I frothed at the mouth as I told Sissily what happened.

After I refused to speak to the two idiots with a death wish on the way back, I stormed through the house and locked myself in the room Amber gave me for the duration of my stay. My best friend convinced me to let her in, and now we sat on the large, comfy bed while I prattled on and on about River and all the ways I wanted to hurt him. Sissily hummed, ah-ed and ooh-ed at all the right places dutifully, as any best friend should, knowing I needed to talk until I was blue in the face so I didn't explode.

"I could've killed them." Repeating it for the fiftieth time didn't make me feel better at all. "Like boom, a pile of bones where Alex and River should stand, anthill style. You saw those shifters in the cornfield. You know?"

"I do." She tucked one leg under her butt and smoothed nonexistent creases on her pants. Her full attention, however, was on me. "It will be a while before I forget that."

"You know what pisses me off?"

"Humm?"

"Knowing my luck, River will make the prettiest, panty melting anthill, and I'll go visit it all the time to pat it and call it cute names. I shit you not, that will happen."

"You're so stupid." Sissily laughed her ass off.

"No, not stupid. I'm fucking angry, Sissily." Curling the comforter in my fists, I breathed through my nose so I didn't smack my magic at my friend. "As in fuming mad, spitting-nails pissed."

"I can tell, girl." Her hand folded over my fist, and she unclenched it one finger at a time. "But look at it from their point of view."

"They have no view, Sissily. Both of those jerks are blind as bats, I'm telling you."

"Blind or not, they trusted you not to hurt them, and you didn't," she pointed out after she was done giggling at my bat comment. I wasn't trying to be funny. I just wanted to strangle Blondie. "To be honest, I kind of agree with River."

"About?" My narrowed glare said to be careful what she said next, but Sissily had never feared me or my fists. She was born without a self-preservation instinct, the poor thing.

"Every time your magic has manifested so far, it's when we are in imminent danger because you are too busy staying alive instead of worrying about everyone else." I already had a hole in her story but waited to hear it all first. "According to what you told me, the same thing happened with Alex because you were freaking out about hurting him until River said he had a way to keep him safe. After that, you lit up like the Fourth of July." Her shoulder twitched in a shrug. "If you are not preoccupied with us, you are perfectly capable of brandishing your power as a weapon."

"You do remember the imp, right?" I smirked smugly, kicking the fragile legs of her claims like a pro. "It used me as a chew toy and popped my boob out, yet no magic came to my rescue. Or yours, for that matter."

"I have a theory about that, too, but you're not going to like it." Since I had no appetite, she plucked a cheese cube from the plate she brought with her and popped it in her mouth. Two more followed until her cheeks were puffed up like a chipmunk. "Umm tost ever," she mumbled through a mouthful of cheese.

"What?" Hunched over, I stared intently at her mouth like a dumbass in hopes of deciphering her words. "What are you? Five? Swallow the damn cheese and speak like a normal person."

I stewed while she took her sweet ass time and chewed the cursed dairy product until it aged in her mouth. My hair had a few gray strands by the time she pushed it down with a heavy sigh. When she just eyed me warily instead of talking, my hand flopped in her face to hurry it up. I would be an anthill myself until she repeated the mumbled words. Hecate help me, the woman was insufferable.

"You trust River." Jutting her chin in her usual expression of stubbornness, she dared me to deny it.

I'd always been happy to oblige.

"Are you allergic to fur?" I grabbed her face between both hands and held her firm, and she struggled as I tugged on the skin under her eyes with my thumbs like I was checking for an illness. "You are feverish and probably hallucinating, that must be it."

"I'm right, and you know it." She zapped me a smidgen just to force me to release her and glared with those blue peepers while she smoothed her hair. "If you made me look like a raccoon, I'll burn a hole in your pants in front of

River." Gingerly, she swiped the tips of her fingers under her eyes to check if I'd smudged her mascara.

"According to your insane theory, I can control my magic if I'm not worried about anyone else. We can test it to see who can burn a bigger hole if you'd like." My syrupy tone earned me an unimpressed scowl. "The last person I trust is Blackman, girl. That's not it. I saw the white glow coming from his hand, so I trusted my eyes not that pigeon. A lesson learned on that front, too."

Lesson 11: *Things are not always what they appear to be in the world of magic. My motto: if it looks like a duck, walks like a duck, and quacks like a duck, then it's a duck, died a sudden and horrible death. The stupid duck turned out to be a goose.*

"Your experience with people is what doesn't trust River. In your head, knowing you as well as I do, you've outlined all the reasons he is not to be trusted. But deep down?" I hated when she slapped me with a knowing look. "In your heart, you know you can trust him. That's why you didn't interrogate him for hours before you accepted it as truth."

"Now I know how others feel when you start preaching nonsense, Miss Know-it-all. I think I'm just overwhelmed and can't think straight." The longer I thought about it, the truer it sounded, unlike Sissily's fantasy world. "As for pretty boy? That guy has more secrets than Danika, I can smell it. The worst thing we can do is place our trust in him. Nothing good will come out of it."

Stretching out across the bed, Sissily clicked her tongue doubtfully. If her plan was to distract me from my anger about what had happened earlier that morning, it actually worked. The clawing fear of all the bad things that could've happened, the biggest of them leaving Amber without a mate and their children without a father, slowly replaced itself with brain-numbing panic that my friend could be right.

River was too handsome for my well being, and for the normal functioning of my brain cells, which flipped the standby button the second he was near. As impossible as it sounded, could it be that he had somehow wiggled his biteable behind under my skin deep enough that I subconsciously trusted him? Apart from Sissily, and now Alex and Amber, I didn't trust anyone. Not even Danika, which had proved to be the smartest decision I'd made.

"You are overthinking it. I can smell something burning all the way over here." Sissily nudged my knee with her thigh. "Let it go, Hazel. Things have a funny way of working themselves out sooner or later. This is not something you can control. At least, I don't think it is."

"What's that supposed to mean? Wing boy is not a cancer I can't cure for Hecate's sake. Of course, I can control it." Wiggling so I could get more comfortable, I gave in to her commands from earlier and reached for the cheese. I thought about all the ways I didn't trust River as I nibbled on it.

"We are witches." My best friend found it necessary to point that out like I'd forgotten what I was. "We don't suffer from human diseases."

"Exactly. So, I can definitely pick and choose who I offer my trust. And River Blackman is not one of them."

"Methinks someone protests too much." She sing-songed and snorted when I smacked her arm. "I never thought I'd be able to tease you about a guy. This is a dream come true for me, so don't be a bitch. Just let me enjoy it."

Tilting her head this way and that, she grimaced. "Well, not more of a bitch than your usual."

"We are not in high school anymore, old fart." Rolling my shoulders didn't relieve the tension I suddenly felt knotting in my muscles there.

"Speak for yourself. I'm still just a young sapling—"

Anything else she wanted to say was cut off when the door of my room burst open, slamming hard against the opposite wall to reveal a frantic-looking Stella as pale as a sheet. The girl was shaking so hard her teeth were audibly chattering, and she was in the beginning stages of a shift. My heart plummeted to my feet, and I jumped to catch her when she pitched forward. Sissily was beside me the next second, and we led the girl to the bed where she dropped because her legs immediately gave out.

"Stella." Kneeling in front of her, I ducked my head to meet her dazed gaze. "Hey, look at me, Stella." Her green eyes, which were so much like her mother's, focused momentarily on mine. "What's wrong, honey? What happened?"

One fat tear rolled down her cheek, and my own hands started trembling.

"The Blackwood pack took my mom." The young girl hiccupped, and more tears spilled down her face. I felt all the blood drain from my head, which made me sway on the floor. "And my baby brother."

Chapter Eighteen

The staircase thudded like a stampede of elephants were running down it as we took the stairs two and three at a time. Stella was beyond listening because she was too terrified for her mother and younger brother, so I left her in my room after we called one of the shifter women that shared the house with us to keep an eye on her. Sissily was right on my heels, barking questions at anyone we passed, but I had a one-track mind. All I wanted to do was find Alex.

My socked feet slid along the wooden floor when I took a sharp turn and bodily opened the door to his office with a hard smack. The alpha's head jerked up when I burst in, and his cold, mismatched gaze locked on mine momentarily. Panting and with my heartbeat in my throat, I opened my mouth to say something, but the subtle shake of his head snapped it shut.

"I know what you're going to say." A deep voice like rocks grinding together came out of his mouth. Alex wasn't talking to me at that moment. His wolf was. "Don't."

He didn't want my apologies, and I totally understood that even if I didn't like it. "What's the plan?"

I had no problem waiting until we brought his family back before I started to grovel. If I lived and had the chance. And maybe it was better not to say a word since I knew he would disagree vehemently with what I had in mind. I, myself, wanted to argue with every thought crossing my panicked brain, but just because I didn't like it, that didn't mean it wasn't right.

"She went to check on the café with one of the beta teams." He gripped the desk with a white-knuckled hold, and the solid oak groaned under the pressure. "They didn't make it there. The car was intercepted soon after they left pack lands. Another team found it empty and flipped on its side. There was no blood in or around it."

"Why was Jack with her?" The name choked me, but I wanted to know. I'd barely seen the boy the whole time I was with them.

Alex's jaw clenched so hard I heard his molars crack.

"He was fussing because he didn't want Amber to leave." River spoke from the door as he swaggered in to join us. "She took him along, not wanting to waste time or hold up the patrol longer than necessary."

"And you didn't go with them, why?" My voice was thick with accusation as I glared at Blondie.

I was fully aware of what I was doing. Instead of blaming myself, I found another target to unload my guilt on. Since I'd met River, I'd pegged him as the perfect person to take the brunt of my anger, and all he had to do was breathe the same air as me. It made me a shitty person, yet I still did it repeatedly. Sissily's displeased press of her mouth told me we were on the same page.

Blackman thinned his lips but didn't indulge me, or my need for an argument.

Grinding my teeth, I waited as he planted himself in front of the desk, full of an authoritative air that was doing its best to strangle me, while I kept sneaking glances like a teenager with a crush. Fuming, I fully turned to Alex so I didn't keep looking at Blondie. For the life of me, I had no idea why he brought out the bitch in me the second he opened his mouth.

"I'd like to help," River told the alpha. "It's a classic manipulation tactic to force you to hand Hazel over, and as appointed guardian, I'd like to deal with this in a quiet manner. If you don't mind."

Bristling that he called himself "guardian" like I was some gate to hell he needed to keep closed, I gnawed on the inside of my cheek. It was either that or cause drama at a very inappropriate time. Which wing man knew, hence why he'd used that particular word.

"What do you have in mind?" To his credit, Alex acted rational, although we could all see him struggling not to shift. There was a wild, ferocious glint in his mismatched gaze that made all the short hairs on my body rise to attention.

"I don't think Amber was the intended target." River glanced at the door when Ace entered, tracking the beta until he stood beside me, and his gaze narrowed when the shifter squeezed my shoulder in reassurance or greeting, but I had no idea which. "From what I've seen so far, they are not big on subtlety. The brutes have no tact. That tells me they thought Hazel was in the car."

"I gathered as much myself," Alex grumbled. "Ace, any news?"

"All teams are ready and waiting on your word." The

beta snapped to attention like a soldier. "We haven't heard anything from Blackwood thus far."

"We are going with you." Denial was written all over the alpha's face even before I was finished talking. "Don't even try it, Alex. If you don't take me with you, I'll just find my own way there."

A menacing growl rumbled in his chest. If he thought that would scare me, he shouldn't have called me a friend that morning. My chin came up a notch and we had a short-lived stare down.

"I will take them with me." Shocked, I gaped at River, but he wouldn't look at me. "I'm guessing you are not planning to simply take your mate and child back. We can return with them while you deal with their alpha."

"I will level them to the ground." Alex's reputation was abundantly clear from that one sentence. A shiver rippled down my vertebrae. "Sissily will come with us. We can use her help." One sharp look and my protest died on my tongue. "You can protect Hazel better if she's the only one you are focused on. We don't know what's waiting for us when we get there."

Wisely, I stayed silent.

All of this was my fault, and I had a feeling if I objected too much, they'd just leave me behind. Sissily took hold of my hand, silently assuring me that everything would be okay, and I squeezed hers in return.

Besides, I had a suspicion my designer shoes wouldn't be very comfortable while walking from pack lands to wherever the Blackwood pack had their snake nest nestled if I tried getting there on my own.

"It's settled then." Blondie tucked a hand in his pocket and nodded sharply at both shifters. "I will follow behind you in my car. All the SUVs are packed."

With slow, deliberate movements, Alex reached back, took hold of his t-shirt, and tugged it over his head. His ebony skin rippled when he rolled his shoulders, barely restraining the violence coming off him in waves. Glowing, mismatched eyes landed on mine, his stone-cold face not showing anything that might be going through his head, but I could take a guess.

"We can mess them up for turning my Mercedes into a harmonica, too," I blurted out for the sake of saying something. I never thought I'd say it, but it was spine-chilling to stare a murderous alpha in the eye. "Alex, I hope Amber—"

"Amber is my mate, and our son is with her. The Blackwood pack should be more afraid of her than me, Hazel." Alex bared his teeth in a perturbing smile. "Let River lead, and don't play a hero. We will teach them a lesson they'll never forget, but it will be all for nothing if you are hurt or taken. Am I clear?"

"I'm just a back-up, got it." My salute earned me a quirked eyebrow.

"Let's move." Alex slapped my shoulder in passing, and we all filed after him toward the front yard where an entire convoy of SUV's were lined up as far as I could see. "I'll see you when we get back."

Sissily gave me a quick hug and rushed to keep up with the long strides of the alpha. I stood watching them pile into the vehicles and reluctantly trailed after Blondie when he cleared his throat. My magic was restless inside me, so I had to remind myself that it was best for everyone if I didn't light up unnecessarily before we reached our destination.

Awkwardly, I slid into the passenger side of River's two-seater and trailed him as he closed the door and jogged around the front to join me. I'd never seen a brand of vehicle like it but didn't want to ask about it. Questions opened conversations, and talking to people humanized them. I had trouble keeping my hands away from Mr. Pigeon as it was, so I didn't need any more reasons to act on my idiotic impulses.

"Amber and the boy will be okay." Misunderstanding the frown twisting my face, Blondie watched me from the side of his peepers.

"I know," I mumbled out loud, but inside?

I didn't doubt that they'd be fine.

But I had no idea if I would be.

Chapter Nineteen

"I'll wait." Tapping his forefingers on the steering wheel, River slouched in the driver seat.

"Obviously." My drawl made his full mouth twitch, so I had to push the rest through clenched teeth. "Unless you know where to find the Blackwood pack."

"I mean, I'll wait for you, but you need to hurry." Slowly, he turned to face me, and his eyes danced with humor on his handsome face. "I'd suggest you go now, or we'll lose them."

"Are you high?" Arching my eyebrow, I shook my head at the idiot. "What are you on about, River?"

"I would be lying if I said I didn't find it absolutely adorable." His peepers dragged down my body until they focused on my feet. "But my guess is you might need shoes if it comes to a fight, firefly. The socks are cute, but not deadly enough."

With a string of curses that would make Danika die from an epilepsy attack and River's laughter follow in my wake, I bolted back inside the house to grab my shoes.

Slipping and sliding on the polished wooden floor, I bruised my hip when I slammed into the doorframe, but at least I was in and out in less than two minutes. Stella was fast asleep on my bed, with the shifter woman we asked to take care of Amber's daughter sitting next to her and petting her hair. The poor girl must've exhausted herself from crying. Seeing her like that sent a sharp stab through my heart.

"Done." River's car rocked when I threw myself inside it with one boot on and the other still clutched in my hand. "Go, go, go."

Slamming on the gas, he tried to see if I could sift through the leather of my seat and end up behind it, but after a moment, I unglued my back and tucked my other boot on. My knee whacked the dashboard, but I kept my mouth shut, although a few choice names for Blondie came to mind.

"Blackwood pack closely resembles the black timber wolves. In contrast to them, as well as any other supernatural that trades shapes, they are much larger. No matter what you compare them with." he said conversationally while expertly maneuvering the tiny vehicle around potholes the size of water wells. Red brake lights from the SUVs were far ahead of us. "The three who attacked us a while back were on the smaller size. Remember that when we face them."

Air filled my lungs so I could reply, but he shifted gears and the back of his hand slid on the outside of my leg. Electricity zapped through me from just above my knee to my heart, which was stuttering faster, and all the way between my thighs. The ass knew exactly what kind of reaction I had to his touch because he appeared a little too focused on the road when I stiffened and stifled a gasp. His fingers tightened on the steering wheel, but he said nothing, thank the goddess.

"You know this how?" My ass wiggled on the leather uncomfortably, and I cleared my throat because I sounded breathy and the tone was too low for my liking. "You're an expert on shifters now?"

"When something attacks me, I make it my business to learn all I can about it." It sounded an awful lot like a reprimand. "While Sissily helped your grandmother search for Leviathan, I looked into the vampires and the Blackwood pack."

"You don't have to give me reports on what you guys were doing while I was caged." Leaning my head back, I stared out the window at the rapidly fading daylight and the way the tops of the trees had a reddish glow around them like they were in flames. "We all do what we need to do given the situation. If I didn't think that I lost my best friend because of my magic, I wouldn't have made the mess a day ago, either."

The convoy had a good start on us, but as soon as we reached the highway, Blondie gunned it and we caught up to them fast. Fields opened on both sides, with an occasional farm here and there placed in the distance. My lids dropped as the comforting hum of the engine filled the silence, until a large, warm had covered mine where it sat limply on my thigh.

"Change is hard, Hazel." River spoke sympathetically and squeezed my hand between his fingers. I struggled to breathe normally. "Unlike the human world, ours is cruel and unforgiving in many ways, but theirs is not. Similar to the humans, we still fear and are distrustful of things we don't understand. Sissily just needed time to process, that's all."

"It sounds like you talk from experience, wing man." Voice raspy, I didn't dare move from fear I'd break the contact. Terrified that I might not break it, if I moved and he kept hold of me, and what would that mean for River and I.

River hummed in acquiescence, his thumb gently grazing a small circle on the back of my hand. I still had my gaze locked on the passing scenery outside the window, but all my focus was on our joined hands resting over my thigh. It seemed he was happy to keep his limb attached to mine as if it was the most natural thing in all the worlds.

On the outside, I made it seem like there was nothing strange about River Blackman holding my hand in his car like we were lovers. Or like I was someone that he deeply cared about. I could've pulled it off, too, if my cursed magic didn't choose that moment to light up like a fucking slot machine in the middle of Vegas announcing a fifty-million-dollar jackpot, the sigils pulsing so fast they almost jumped out of my skin.

"Sorry." He most definitely did not look sorry at all and lingered longer than necessary before taking back his warm, calloused palm.

With my heart beating in my throat and my hand frozen the way he left it like I was too afraid to move it, I cleared my throat. "If you want people to believe that you are sorry, you'll need to rearrange your features to match your words, Blackman."

"Would you like me to tell you I'm not?" With a daring glint in his knowing gaze, he moved his attention from the road to me.

"I'd like you to watch the road, thank you very much." Huffing in indignation, I hoped he couldn't see the heat rising in my cheeks. "I might have magic now, but I'd like not to test the boundaries of my mortality, mm-kay?"

"As the lady wishes." Jerk McJerkenson chuckled, purposely taking his time to face forward. "What will it take, Hazel?"

His knuckles where he rested his hand on the stick shift kept brushing against my leg, and the change in conversation was giving me whiplash. "You'll need to be more specific. I have no idea what you're asking."

"To trust me," he said simply. "Or to not distrust me, however you want to phrase it."

"Trust is not given, Blackman." Shifting to get more comfortable, I was grateful my hormones took a hike thanks to the change of direction in our conversation. "It's earned."

"Truth. But how does one earn something if he doesn't get the opportunity to do so?"

"Reallyyyy?" This was a subject I had studied my whole life thanks to lies, deceits, manipulations, and all sorts of fuckery people had tried to pull on me. "Hmmm, let me think." Tapping a finger on my lip, I pretended to think. "Would you like me to list all the opportunities you've had so far but chose not to tell me the truth? I'll let you know, Sissily is the queen of listing shit, with a perfected finger counting tactic, all which she uses against me. I've learned from the best."

"I never lied." Yet his knuckles turned white on the steering wheel. Would you look at that? "Omitting is not the same as lying, and you know it. You and I are alike in many ways. Surely you can understand where I'm coming from."

"I know nothing about you, Blackman, while you hold enough info to screw my life ten ways to Sunday. You inserted yourself in my existence out of nowhere, and now you're buried neck deep. I, on the other hand, apart from the fact that you turn into a goose on occasion, know nothing. My lack of information when it comes to you is astonishing. Trust doesn't work that way, I'm afraid."

"I beg to differ. You know almost all there is about me," River muttered under his breath. When I opened my mouth to protest, he waved me off in annoyance. "Sissily told you most of it."

"Huh? You think too highly of yourself if you think we talk about you." Internally I was freaking out. Shit. Did he eavesdrop while we gossiped about him in my room?

"Don't patronize me, firefly. The bond between the two of you is awe inspiring. If one knows something, the other one does, too. And vice versa." My mouth snapped shut because there was nothing I could say to that. The death grip he had on the steering wheel loosened, and he tapped a forefinger on it as if debating something. "Very well. Let's make it fair, for mutual trust's sake."

My heart jumped to the roof of my mouth before dropping to splatter at my feet.

"I'm sure Sissily told you that Danika agreed to help me find my mother in exchange for my help in protecting you." A muscle spasmed on the side of his jaw. "What she doesn't know ... what no one knows and I'm trusting you with is ..." He took a deep breath as if he was about to deliver grave news.

"We—" I didn't get a chance to stop him. He spoke over me.

"My father never gave his consent for conceiving a child with an angel." All the blood drained from my head, and a whooshing sound filled my ears. River kept talking. "He raised me, although he never wanted my existence. My father is a very good man who never joined a coven, all so he could protect me. I'm not searching for my mother for sentimental reasons, Hazel. I want to find the bitch so I can kill her."

"Why are you telling me this," I breathed through numb lips.

"Because I'm going to need your help." He didn't look at me, but I felt his damn gaze drilling into the core of my being.

Chapter Twenty

"Sissily," I hissed as I darted through the trees in search of my best friend. "Sissily!"

Screw orders and everything else, I needed to talk to her like yesterday. After the bomb River dumped on me, all I could do was blink and breathe in the car. The moment we reached our destination and his two-seater was parked behind the last SUV in a line of many, I was out of that bitch like my ass was on fire in search for Sissily.

"Will you stop yelling," my friend hissed as she rushed to meet me.

"I was whisper-shouting. There's a difference." Never missing an opportunity to needle her, I bared my teeth. Blondie was right on my heels, but I ignored the dumbass. Who in their right mind dumps something like that on another person?

A jerk. That was who.

"What's wrong?" Sissily took hold of my shoulders and eyed me up and down. "You okay?"

"Oh, I'm wonderful, but I'm so glad you asked," I piped

in cheerfully. Good thing we were all parked a mile or so away from the Blackwood pack lands because I was ready to scream. "Pulling off a rescue mission, dealing with a dumbass, planning a murder. How about you? Are you having fun?"

"Wha-what?" She probably thought a screw had loosened in my head with the way she was eyeing me before glancing at Blondie over my shoulder. "What did you do to her, River?"

"Nothing," Blondie answered in a flat tone.

"I don't think it's nothing." Sissily searched my face, no doubt seeing the crazed glint in my peepers. "I think you broke her." She glowered at him.

"We can discuss this later, ladies. The alpha might need our help." Using logic against us, he waved his hand to indicate we should get moving.

"Go, I'll tell you later." Reluctantly, I decided that River's murder plan could wait. "But, if pretty boy ends up as an anthill, know that it wasn't my fault."

With a shake of her head and her ponytail lashing at the back of her head, she ran to join the shifters ahead of us. Maybe one day I'd be trusted not to kill everyone, and they'll invite me into the front lines, too. Until then, I had no choice but to stick to potential killers. The humans back in the days had one of those, too. A pretty face that killed so many, but no one had ever suspected what kind of a twisted psycho rested under it until it was too late.

"Hazel." With a sigh, River glued himself so close behind me I could feel the heat from his skin. "I'm not asking you to kill anyone. What I do with my mother is on me."

"So, you were asking me what? To compare knitting patterns with her while you stab her in the back?" The glare

I threw at him over my shoulder would've made anyone else run for the hills.

River smiled, just a small twitch of his lips. "Just to have my back, that's all." Ducking to pass a low branch, he glided smoothly through the trees. "She's an angel. I don't want you to get hurt, but I want to be prepared for any scenario."

"How does that even work?"

It didn't escape my notice that I was a hypocrite. While I preached to Blondie about trust, the first time he'd shared something with me, I ran to Sissily so I could blab it out. Not that River blinked an eye or anything, but still. Maybe it was time to rethink things. The night that cursed book opened the floodgates to my magic wasn't the only thing that had changed in my life. I let people in where I normally would've balked at the idea. It wasn't just me and Sissily against the world anymore. We had more people in our corner.

Could River be one of those?

"How does what work?" River swatted another low-hanging branch out of his way.

Lost in my thoughts and distracted by Blondie prowling through a forest dressed in pants and a button down, I didn't move fast enough. The damn tree reached for my hair, and it got tangled there while prickly thorns stabbed my scalp. Flailing didn't help much either, especially when Blondie snorted. I had to stay still while he took his time and detangled my hair from the vegetation, all the while I pretended him being that close didn't affect me.

"This." Using the conversation to divert my attention from his body and scent, I flicked a finger between us. "How is it I'm not dead on contact? That's the first lesson they teach us before we can walk. Stay away from Fallen and Angels. One touch, and you're done. But you've touched me, and I'm still kicking."

"It's used as a caution, everything they say about any celestial being." His face was tilted up as he gently extracted my strands from the branch. He was focused on it as if it was the most important job in the world to have. "Angels, as well as a Fallen, need intent before their magic can work because it's so potent. Whatever, or whoever, created them didn't want any accidents to happen, I guess."

"You're saying they've killed everyone that touched them because they felt like it?" I found my fingers pressing to his sternum, and I snatched my hand back. What in the actual fuck was happening to me around River? "On purpose?" I blinked when I heard the awe in my tone.

"I thought you might find that very appealing." River grinned down at me, and my breath ended up stuck in my throat. "Yes, they chose to kill anyone who dared touch them. That's why nothing will happen if you ..." His voice deepened, and the smile slipped from his lips. "If you want to touch me."

My lungs screamed from lack of oxygen as I stared into his smoldering gaze. A lock of his blond hair fell forward, and unable to resist, my hand lifted to his face and brushed it aside. The tips of my fingers grazed his skin, and with a barely audible groan, he closed his eyes.

I swayed toward him as if pulled by the same invisible thread that tugged at my chest every time River was near. As his head lowered further, his mouth was close enough for me to feel his breath ghosting over my own. There was no doubt I would've kissed him if that first scream didn't pierce the night and make me jerk away from him.

"Shit."

Calling myself all sorts of stupid and a few other words

I'd never say internally or out loud, I made a mad dash in the direction of the sound. River stayed level with me, although he could've gotten there sooner. All he had to do was sprout his wings, but he didn't. I refused to think about what that meant and what could've happened if we hadn't been interrupted. Feet punching the ground covered in fallen leaves and twigs, I pumped my arms to add more speed.

Pulses of golden glow blinked across the trees and undergrowth while shrubbery and low branches tugged at my clothes and scraped my skin. When we reached the clearing, I skidded to a stop because I couldn't understand what I was looking at. Gray wolves were slicing into much larger black ones, using teeth, claws, and anything else they could find. They even went as far as flinging dead or unconscious shifters at each other. Alex stood in the middle of the animals in all his human glory, bare chested, spitting mad, and tearing into anything that moved with his bare hands. The alpha was literally ripping wolves twice his size limb from limb and bathing in thick sprays of blood that gushed from his victims.

Sissily angled herself a step behind the alpha, her body partially hidden by his larger bulk, and she flung bolts of magic at the Blackwood pack like it was going out of style. My best friend's petite form made her look like a pixie, with her long blonde hair and wide, expressive blue eyes, compared to the enormous alpha and his glistening, ebony skin and tree-trunk arms.

"Stop, or the bitch dies." A burly man with a shaggy beard that reached his chest stepped out from the tree line ahead of us, yanking a disheveled Amber alongside him by her upper arm. His voice carried despite the snarls and howls echoing around us.

The biggest shock of my life was delivered in the form of a gigantic alpha covered in blood like war paint, the coppery, sticky liquid dripping from his body in thick ropes, and it came when he laughed his ass off as his eyes landed on the psycho holding his wife hostage. Not just his wife, I noticed. Amber was clutching Jack to her, his face hidden by a cloud of fire-red corkscrews. River made a grab for me and bodily carried me out of sight.

"Blackwood, I see you are still dumb as fuck." Alex guffawed while the other man silently snarled at him. "I believe you've taken my mate, but you haven't met her."

Amber lifted her head and locked her gaze on the alpha. The next thing happened in a blur. She pushed Jack away from her, and the kid bolted toward his father, shifting mid-run, and as a small pup, he darted around anyone who tried to stop him. Alex snatched him in his arm and tucked him to his massive chest, still chuckling like a loon. Sissily attempted a dash for Amber, but the alpha threw his free arm out and stopped her.

In the place where Amber stood, a ball of magic exploded, and a slim red wolf jerked its head back and mournfully howled at the now-dark sky. River's sharp intake of breath along with all the wolves present taking a step back in surprise told me I was missing something.

"I don't get it ..." I started saying to Blondie when the small wolf pounced like gravity didn't exist and ripped the throat out of the man next to it before I even had time to blink. "Well, shit."

Lesson 12: *If you ever see a red wolf, don't just run. Run, scream your ass off, and do it all in zig-zag style. That way, there will be zero-point-zero-one chance of survival.*

Chapter Twenty-One

We saw the black, monstrous wolf a second too late.

River was too busy trying to drag me back the same way we'd come, and as you might've guessed, I struggled like a cat dumped in water, claws and all. What was his problem, anyway? We were the victors, and I didn't even get the chance to turn some of those jerks into anthills thanks to the touchy-feely crap he'd pulled back there. I'd say that counted as a win.

Both of us froze when a low, menacing growl came from beside us, and twigs cracked under the massive weight of the Blackwood shifter. Two more dark shapes spread out from behind him, all of them with their heads lowered and ears pinned to the back of their skulls. A red glow lit up their eyes like hellish lanterns on their snarling faces, and my heart skipped a beat as I watched saliva dribble from their bared, sharp teeth.

Blondie decided to continue being an ass by tucking me behind him like some damsel in distress. Unfortunately for him, he was the one who taught me how to somewhat control my magic, so grinning like a mad woman, I sent a zap right to his biteable butt. He scowled at me over his shoulder after yelping and jumping a foot off the ground.

For the record, no, I wasn't an idiot. Aware of the three shifters ready to rip us to shreds, I simply wasn't as worried as I should've been. Wing man proved he could stand his ground with a horde of demons facing him. Against three wolves, no matter how large and strong, it was like bringing a knife to a gunfight, as the humans liked to say.

Usually, a time always came when being too cocky brought karma knocking on the door.

Which was the case at that moment.

River's eyes widened momentarily, and before I could turn to see what had spooked the arrogant man, he grabbed my wrist and tugged me in front of the wolves. The shifters pounced without any warning, and I ended up rolling around in the dirt to avoid seeing my internal organs decorating the outside of my body. Grinding my teeth, I was ready to tear River a new one, but my anger fizzled into dust when I saw what he faced.

Two shade demons circled around him, their arms long past their knees and their jaw stretched out of their elongated, bold heads to almost reach their stomachs. At around eight feet or so, their willowy frames swayed in a nonexistent wind like snakes. These particular demons were not physically strong, which actually made them a worse adversary to face because they screwed with your mind. Liars, witches liked to call them, because they manipulated your thoughts until you went completely mad and killed everyone around you. Poor Blondie better call on his strong will if he'd like to defeat Python's spirits of lying.

"Watch out," I shouted when a third came from behind River, one arm outstretched to touch his shoulder.

He danced away, but that was all I saw because I had to keep the shifters off me. Two of the wolves snapped their jaws an inch from my face and jugular, which I barely escaped with a well-placed round-house kick and a burst of magic I used like a rope to smack one across the snout. Shouts, roars, and howls came from the clearing where we left Alex and Sissily, and although I wanted to rush to them and see if they needed help, I couldn't.

Crouched low, I mimicked the movement of the black beasts when they tried to spread out and corner me from three sides. Sigils enthusiastically pulsing under my skin, I chose a different approach to a fight for the first time. Instead of using my fighting skills, I would only use my powers. With that in mind, I focused on the magic churning inside me and flicked both wrists at the shifters.

Blasts of bright light streamed from my fingertips, one too wide and cracking a tree in half, but the other met its mark. The magic wrapped around the wolf like a rope and circled its neck, spitting and hissing as it ate through fur, skin, and bone. The wolf whined and howled to no avail until its body dropped on the forest floor with a dull thump, the head rolling away from it. Not a drop of blood spilled on the ground. With one down and two standing, I turned toward them, wiggling my fingers as a threat.

Trees rustled and cracked behind me where River fought the shades. Their hissed whispers tried to push into my mind, but I repeated very loudly in my head, "Not happening, nope, not happening," so I could focus on myself rather than whatever lies they spat at me.

One of the remaining wolves made a move to jump right, and I followed, but it changed directions at the last moment and his teeth sank into my side. One sharp tooth pressed deep enough I felt it scrape over my hip bone, and stars bloomed in front of my eyes. The scream I wanted to stifle ripped from my throat and echoed across the forest like a cloud of scared birds bursting from the treetops. My hand flopped in a wide arc, sending dark puffs of magic with blood red veins around me, which spread like a sheet.

That was when I heard it.

The voices were faint, and they didn't use words. More like the tone was conveying their intent. Mind-numbing pain spread through me, and the stronger it was, the louder they got. In the meantime, the second wolf took the opportunity to tackle me, and only my hold on his snout prevented him from chewing off my face. In the back of my mind, I knew the voices wanted to help me, and with my blood soaking into the dry soil, I gave in to them.

River frantically calling my name was a distant noise in the background.

Warmth poked me where my body was mushed in the bed of fallen leaves. At first, I thought it was my blood that had leaked from where the shifter held onto my side like a dog with a bone, but when it started spreading, my half-lidded eyes snapped open. The ground was shivering violently, and panic gripped me because I felt another wave of power ready to explode, and this one would kill friend and foe alike. Weakly, I pressed the palm of my hand between the foliage until my fingers dug into the dry soil.

Then the forest came alive.

Thick, gnarly roots from the trees shot upward, bursting from the forest floor like they had a mind of their own. Whipping wildly, they swung above my head before crashing around me. One caught the shifter straddling me and took him in the air before slamming him as if he was a doll in a pissed-off toddler's hand. The wolf shivered and shifted to a naked man who never stood up. Through the middle of his chest, a young tree was already growing, becoming bigger with each passing second.

A large tree lowered, looming above me, and I flinched because I expected it to crush me as well. It stopped so close that I could've touched its leaves if I reached out a hand. The crown of it rustled in anticipation, leaving me bewildered as to how I knew that. Then his branch, which was wider than my body, swung down and pulverized the black wolf who still had his teeth still inside my flesh. The sharp teeth were yanked out, and I cried out, but at least the shifter was gone.

In a daze, I watched the forest return to its original inanimate state until all was silent, apart from my sawing breath. My skin was knitting together, burning as the muscle regenerated itself like nothing I'd ever felt before. Dark spots danced in front of my eyes from blood loss, yet I flipped first on my back then on my side, needing to see if River was okay. My heart skipped a beat when he dropped on his knees and gathered me in his arms, squeezing so hard I whimpered.

"Sissily ... Alex ..." Words wouldn't form in my mouth because my tongue was too thick and dry. "Please ..."

"They are fine, Hazel." River rocked me back and forth, his hands running all over me to check for injuries. I would've told him they were healed if I could. "No one expected demons to attack here. You saved them all." A strange glint entered his gaze that pooled dread in my belly. "Where are you hurt?"

"No," was all I could croak.

"So much blood," River kept muttering the same thing under his breath. "There is too much blood."

Following his gaze, I feebly glanced at my exposed skin. The sigils that blinked happily under it could barely be noticed. Ever since my magic awoke, I'd never seen how my flesh looked without them, and at that moment, emptiness yawned inside me. I didn't look whole. It was like a limb was missing without the symbols that usually etched themselves on me in mockery. Whatever they were, I needed them back.

"Hazel," Sissily's shout followed, and the thumping of more than just two feet followed until faces appeared above me where I was curled to River's chest. My best friend's worried gaze looked too big for her face. Alex loomed, too, with Jack in his arms and Amber tucked to his side. Ace was there as well, the beta clenching his fists to keep his hands to himself, no doubt.

Hysterical laughter bubbled inside me, and I somehow croaked it out. "Not ... dying."

"You better not be, Hazel Byrne, because I'd find a way to bring you back so I could kill you myself." Sissily bared her teeth at me like a feral animal.

The darkness beckoned.

"Deal," I whispered, but I wasn't sure I said it out loud. Chances were I'd lost my mind because I could've sworn I heard River whisper for my ears only.

"Sleep, firefly. I'll protect you with my life."

But that'd be dumb. Right?

Chapter Twenty-Two

Dead.

I must've been dead, or otherwise I was about to pitch a witch. Something was licking my face like a fucking popsicle, and I could feel the drool sticking to my skin from my chin to my forehead, the tongue snagging on the tip of my nose in passing. Revulsion tossed the contents of my stomach around like a tornado, and I had to keep my mouth shut so I didn't projectile vomit all over myself.

At least I was stretched out on something soft.

"Always look on the bright side of things," Sissily repeatedly said to me in hopes to drill it in my grumpy head. Bright side, my ass. I'd liked to see what she'd find good about being licked. Before I was misunderstood, I'd like to mention that, just like any other woman, I was all for licking. Hell to the fucking yeah. Be my guest. Bon Appetit.

Just not this type of slobbering.

My eyes were glued shut and, short of tearing them up, there was no way they'd open. Tried, failed, and not doing it again. Both arms were limp next to my body and tied to something since I couldn't even flinch. I had the desire to ask whoever had done that to me what would happen if I suddenly had to scratch my ass. Would they do it for me?

Internally screaming, all I wanted was to know what in all hell was going on.

Did I die for real?

Was this my Hell where my face was being disgustedly licked to the bone?

It was. Wasn't it?

"She's waking up." A soft feminine murmur reached my insane, panicked brain.

"Move Jack away from her. The poor girl can't breathe." Another woman spoke, her tone reproachful yet concerned.

I figured that little fucker had used this opportunity to do it when I couldn't push him away. Every time Jack shifted and I'd been around him, he'd try to lick my face for whatever reason. That was why I stayed as far away from the little shit as I could. I had a suspicion the tiny alpha wolf liked the taste of makeup, as disputable as that sounded. Not that I'd dare say anything to Amber or Alex. What if it killed him? I'd rather not be held accountable for that shit storm, thank you very much.

"Hazel, can you hear me?" The moment River Blackman spoke and his baritone vibrated in my chest like he was a damn gong, something became clear.

I was as naked as the day I was born, and only a very thin sheet covered me. With River goddess damn Blackman in the cursed room. I wouldn't trust myself around him if I was mummified and it took him half a year to unwrap me. Naked? Oh, hell to the no.

My eyes popped open, and I became animated all at once. With the sheet clutched to my chest, I scrambled on the bed, crab-walking backward until my spine cracked the headboard. Sissily squealed before she pressed her mouth into a disapproving line, but the bitch could get in line. Friends never let friends sprawl naked and get licked in the face with wing man in the room. Like, ever.

"Out." My hand shot up, and one trembling finger pointed at the closed door of my room.

A few pairs of peepers blinked at me. If they didn't wipe the flabbergasted expressions off their face, I'd make sure each of their eyes ended up in one of Danika's jars. On full display, front row and everything.

"I'd say she's awake," River droned flatly, unimpressed by my hostility. He wasn't the one with all his bits airing freely, so he could shove his attitude up his butt.

"Yup," I chirped and gave him a crazed smile. "Awake, alive, and ready to tackle the day. Bright-eyed and bushy-tailed. That's me. Now get the hell out." My finger wiggled to get his attention.

Nothing.

Jack, however, used the distraction to slither out of Amber's hold and jump me. The kid was nine, for Hecate's sake. Someone should've taught him licking was a big no-no until he was of age, and even then, the face was not the way to go. How old did they need to be before one could fight them? Ten? The young wolf's birthday was coming up soon, I was sure of it.

"Sorry, Hazel." Amber snatched the wolf resembling a poodle off the bed. "When he shifts, this is his way of showing affection." Her sheepish smile made me feel guilty for my thoughts, and the kid called me out on them by yelping and lolling his tongue playfully to the side.

I really was an asshole.

"Here." Sissily stuck a straw in my mouth before I could protest, and I glared at her scowl as I sucked on the water. It was her way of shutting me up before I shoved my foot deeper in my mouth. "I hoped you'd wake up with some of that bitchiness gone, but the stars were not aligned in my favor."

"Thank you." Picking my battles, I didn't dignify that with a reply. "How are you and Jack, Amber? I'm really sorry this happened to you because of me."

Since Blondie made himself comfortable in the one wingback chair in the room, I decided to ignore him. Without attention, he'd leave eventually.

"Nonsense." The older woman waved me off as if they'd taken her on vacation and not been holding her against her will. "With Alex being so overprotective, I rarely get to let my wolf out to play." A mischievous smile lit up her face. "She loved it, although it didn't last nearly as long as she would've liked."

"Drink this, too." Sissily shoved another straw at me like some glass tyrant, but this time I dodged it and eyed the liquid warily.

"What is it?" It was not water, that much was clear. Or cloudy as far as liquids went.

"Just drink it, Hazel. I'm not in the mood to beg you to do what's good for you." With a sigh, she nudged the straw at my mouth.

Rearing my head back and careful not to drop the sheet, I narrowed my gaze on her. "Why do you insist on feeding me grass juice every time I don't feel well, or am I injured?"

Amber started laughing heartedly, and even River snorted, but my friend only pressed her mouth firmer. "It's tea," she informed me.

"Were all the herbs green when you made it?" Sissily knew how much I disliked tea, especially those made to make you feel better. All her concoctions tasted awful, and there were no exceptions. I'd never say no if she offered me booze to get me on my feet, for example, but no, she fancied herself a hedge witch or something.

"Yes, now drink it."

"So, grass juice, as I said." Slapping her hand away, I chortled along with Amber, who was wiping tears away with the back of her hand. That was when I noticed how pale my friend was. "What's wrong?" I snatched her arm when she tried to pull away." Sissily, talk, or I'll make you."

"You scared me, you ass," she shouted so loud my shoulders reached my ears. "Again!"

"I know, and I'm sorry." On a deep exhale, I dragged her until she crawled on the bed next to me. Wrapping her in a hug and careful not to show my boobs to River, I squeezed her as hard as I could. Which wasn't much since my limbs felt like limp noodles. "I swear I'm not doing it on purpose."

"Right." She snort-sobbed on my shoulder. "I'll die young just from watching you trying to kill yourself."

"They spoke to me, girl." It was easy to ignore the other two people in the room. "I didn't think anything of it since I was bleeding to death anyway."

"I knew you were hurt," River hissed and jumped off the chair. "How?"

The next thing I knew, he grabbed the sheet and yanked on it to bare the side of my body to him. By no means was I a prude, but buy a girl a dinner first. Jerk. My legs scissored, and he tucked his groin away before I smacked the ball of my foot in his jingle-berries, which allowed me to wrap the sheet around me like a burrito.

"What in Hecate's name is wrong with you?" I shouted at him. "You don't get to see my bare ass or my vajayjay without permission. Actually, scratch that. You won't see them, ever."

"I'm not trying to gawk at your naked body, woman. I was trying to see if there was any indication of an injury left, so don't be absurd." But his voice had gone husky, and his gaze was scorching when it flicked to mine. Three sets of female eyes watched him fidget. "Oh, for goodness sake." Blondie threw both his arms in the air. "She healed faster than anyone I've ever seen. I thought I'd imagined the Blackwood wolf tearing her side open. I was worried I was going insane."

"Nope, not insane. It just turned you into a creep." I had to bite my lip not to chortle in his face when Jack, who'd escaped his mother yet again, lifted a leg and peed on River's foot.

"Unbelievable," Blondie groaned while I snickered, but my joy was short-lived.

Sissily used the situation to her advantage and forced the straw between my lips. My flat stare told her everything I thought about it, but I drank the disgusting thing dutifully.

"It'll restore your energy much faster." My friend explained as if that would change the fact that she was as stubborn as me when she made her mind up about something.

I'd never tell her, but it did work. Tingles started at the tips of my fingers and toes, but soon they spread everywhere. Since I'd woken up, I had pointedly avoided looking at my skin, but even from my periphery, I knew the sigils were faint. The more I gulped from the grass juice, the brighter they became.

"What did you put in this?" Frowning into the now-empty glass, I flicked my gaze to my friend.

"The color is returning to her face," Amber muttered,

crowding closer to peer at me from the side of the bed. Even River forgot about his drenched pant leg and shoe as he observed me. "Her Fae magic is reacting to the herbs you used, Sissily. Well done, dear."

My friend blushed to her roots at the phrase. Sissily never knew how to accept a compliment without feeling awkward, which I'd never understood. The woman was amazing. Smart, talented, loyal, kind, driven, and very beautiful inside and out. She had it all, yet at the slightest compliment, she looked like she was ready to bolt or dig a hole to hide in. It was mind boggling.

"I mixed ginseng, peppermint, and sage, but it didn't feel like enough. I added ashwagandha to give it a kick, too." Her shoulder twitched in a shrug. "I never thought of mixing those together, but it felt right."

"It worked." Amber squeezed my friend's upper arm affectionately. "You'll have to mix some for me, too. Someone always needs a boost around here. Do you think it'll work on shifters?"

"I don't see why not?" I pointedly locked eyes with Amber, remembering what the alpha had said about their origins. If the tea worked on me, it must be the same for the shifters. "Did anyone get hurt last night?" The sun was coming through the window, telling me I had a full night's sleep.

"A few cuts and scratches, but nothing serious." Amber darted her green gaze awkwardly to River.

"What is it you're not telling me?" Instantly, I was on alert.

"It was two days ago, not last night, Hazel." Blondie spoke cautiously. "We couldn't wake you until you stirred on your own not long ago."

That explained why Sissily was freaked out, and I felt

horrible all over again for being the reason she'd gone through all of it. The worst possible thing she could've done was become my friend, yet the stubborn witch always had my back, through thick and thin. I hugged her again, in gratitude this time, my grip much stronger than before.

"Thank you for the tea," I told her earnestly.

"You mean for the grass juice." Snorting, my friend jabbed me in the ribs with her finger.

A soft knock on the door had all of us turning to face it, and as soon as I called for whoever it was to enter, Ace filled the doorway. "Alex wanted you to join him in the office." He spoke to Amber, but his eyes widened when he saw me awake. "Oh, you are awake, Hazel. If you can, maybe you should come, too."

"Anything the matter?" Amber scooped Jack up, who was already headed for the open door.

"Danika is here." Ace's declaration made me groan.

"Hazel is an ass," Jack, who'd shifted back into an annoying butt-naked nine-year-old, announced loudly. Obviously turning into a wolf never stopped a child from overhearing things they shouldn't. My grandmother might've had plans for my broodmare status to continue the Byrne bloodline, but I had every intention of staying childless for the next few centuries, if I survived that long.

"You bet your cute bare butt that I am an ass," I told Jack with a proud grin, and I laughed with everyone else, but inside I was fuming.

What new clusterfuck did Danika bring to my plate now?

Chapter Twenty-Three

"...couldn't be sure, but everything points at Destin at this moment," Danika was saying to Alex when I joined them.

Everyone had left my room, so I had the opportunity to dress instead of walking around like some roman goddess wrapped in only a sheet, but that meant I'd missed half of the conversation.

"Hazel, I'm happy to see that you are well." Cold emerald eyes perused me from head to toe like a laser security device.

"Danika." Biting back the other words I wanted to say, I focused on what I'd heard as I walked in. "What does the master vampire have to do with all of this? Apart from sending his lackeys to attack everyone, I mean?"

"Straight to the point." Alex chuckled, and I smiled thinly when I saw the concern he didn't voice in his gaze.

"We've already wasted enough time on nonsense while they come at us from all sides, don't you think?" Sissily was curled on the overstuffed loveseat, so I plonked down next to her, avoiding my grandmother's intent stare.

"Time passed more than it should've, yes, but I wouldn't say it was wasted." The alpha leaned back on his chair and stroked Amber's thigh where she was perched on the armrest next to him. "Meanwhile, we learned many things we didn't know."

"Is this where you remind me that a good predator is an informed predator?" I wiggled to angle myself strangely just so I could pointedly avoid not just Danika's but River's peepers, too.

"Not just a good predator, but an alive one, too." Alex grinned like a proud parent at me. I couldn't help it when I snickered along with Sissily.

"Listen, Alex." Scrubbing a hand over my face, I sighed into my palm. "No matter how many times I say sorry, it never seems like enough. None of this was your problem, but we ... I brought it to your doorstep, and your mate and child almost ended up hurt. Maybe it'll be better if I go back home after everything."

Danika wisely stayed silent, and I knew the alpha called everyone because whatever news she brought was important, but I had to say my peace. The more I thought about it, the more the guilt drilled a hole the size of Texas into my gut.

"According to the recent development, I would have to disagree with you, young lady." Alex kept eye contact so I could see the truth in his mismatched gaze. A tremor raked my spine since Amber was nodding from next to him with a grave expression on her sweet face. "It would appear whoever is behind this started from the top and plans to follow the food chain until the field is left open for the picking, for them alone."

I blinked.

"As I was saying ..." Danika draggedher calculating

gaze from me back to the alpha. "Destin is in close cahoots with the demons. We thought it had been isolated nests of his kind using the price on Hazel's head to attack the coven. The mistake was mine for jumping to conclusions. One I have no intention of repeating."

"Why would he kick the hornet's nest?" Alex leaned his forearms on the desk and clasped his hands in front of him until the skin on his knuckles turned lighter. "As the Master vampire of the northeast region, he had it as good as you and me. The same as Leviathan, too."

"Speaking of which." I finally looked at my grandmother, who sat ramrod straight like a queen. "Did you find your buddy, the Fallen? What did he have to say for himself?"

"He must've been promised something better than the agreement we had between each other." Danika ignored me like I hadn't spoken. "Which brings to question if the angels have decided to return. Or better, if the Fae are about to crawl out of their hole."

"Why is no one involving the magi police?" My question was for Alex since he was the only one listening to what I had to say. "We do all their dirty work, yes, but they should get off their pompous asses and help clean up this mess."

You could hear a pin drop.

"I don't get it," I told the room at large, speaking to no one in particular.

"The magi police do not look kindly on mixed bloodlines or combined powers." River was the one who took pity on me. Judging by his own mixed bloodline, I could see how he would know. "When something attacks me, I make it my business to learn all I can about it." His words from the car, which felt like a lifetime ago, ping-ponged in my head.

"Most of their agents are either vampires or mages. There will be no help coming from them."

"So, no matter what way we look at it, we are screwed either way? Is that what you're telling me?"

"Whichever way we turn and however we look at it, the demons are in the middle of it all." Danika smoothed invisible wrinkles on her black, floor-length dress. "I've exhausted all my resources in search of Leviathan, with nothing to show for it. It's like he's vanished from the face of the realm."

"Hazel should know what we found after the battle with the Blackwood pack." Amber nudged her mate, and I smiled at her gratefully.

"Yes, my love. She needs to know." Rubbing his forehead harshly like he was developing a headache, Alex never looked so tired before. Not even when he had his t-shirt inside out. The proud alpha seemed to have aged since the first time I saw him ripping wolves in half with his bare hands and sitting behind his desk.

"Hit me with it, big guy." Hoping to make him smile, I curled my fingers in invitation. "It can't be as bad as what we just spoke about." The flattening of his mouth said it might be worse.

My heart skipped a beat.

"None of the Blackwood pack survived." I felt all the blood rush from my face. "More than half of them had demonic spirits leaving their corpses the minute they died."

"Possessions," I whispered faintly, and Sissily hummed from next to me, only adding to the dread.

"Possessions," Alex confirmed with a sharp nod. "Which tells me that the vampires might be carrying passengers, as well. They sure fought like they did in the attack on the coven."

"What are we waiting for, then?" I searched all their faces. "We should go directly to them and deal with this once and for all." When no one spoke, anger surged through my numb limbs. "I'm not planning on living my whole life looking over my shoulder or hiding like a coward. One of you might as well just kill me now. If we go to them, we either fix this or we don't. I die, or whoever pulls the strings dies. It's quite simple, really."

"You staying alive now is more important than ever," Danika told me primly. It only irked me more.

"Oh, crap. That screwed up your plans, didn't it, Grandmother?"

"Don't be immature, Hazel Byrne." Sniffing haughtily, she stared down her nose at me. "I've gone to great lengths to keep you alive, so don't make me regret it."

Judging by the pity I saw on everyone's faces, she was already regretting it plenty. I just didn't point it out to her. It was written all over her face for the world to see. It hurt like a bitch, but I pushed it out of my mind, taking strength from Sissily's squeeze on my arm.

"I say we stick to the plan." Alex cut off the stare-down between Danika and me. "It's as good as any."

My grandmother nodded once, but as always, I was left out of the loop and had to ask, "Which is?"

"The attacks on the pack lands to get to Hazel follow a pattern. Our teams know ahead of time exactly when and where they'll happen." The alpha locked gazes with River for a long moment in some silent conversation the rest of us were not privy to. "We will capture one of the vampires if we can't get hold of a demon. It'll make things slightly more complicated, but not by much thanks to what we now know of Hazel's magic."

"Hold on, hold on." My hand rose in protest, and I

turned between the two men in the room. "What do you mean 'what we know of Hazel's magic?' Hazel"—My thumb jabbed at my chest— "knows nothing of her weirdo magic apart from that it kills people. In very disturbing ways, I might add."

"That's what we need it to do." Alex smiled as if that should've made me feel better. "The wolves we killed showed nothing, but those that your magic killed released their demonic spirits or shades. If we capture one, we can interrogate it."

"Do I have a say in this?" But it was a useless question. I knew I didn't. "Whatever, fine. I'll do whatever you need me to do, but let me tell you all one thing: if you can't contain that thing and it attacks or possesses someone, I'm out. I'm not getting blamed for this, too."

"No one is blaming you for anything, Hazel." Danika sounded put out.

"You blame me for breathing instead of my mother." It was out before I could stop it.

Danika Byrne, queen bitch of the Gatekeeper's coven, had nothing to say to that.

Shocker, I knew.

Alex cleared his throat awkwardly, and I almost laughed. "That's where Mr. Blackman comes. If the demonic entity proves difficult to contain, he can destroy it or back you up, Hazel."

Understanding dawned, and my eyes locked on River. I knew the accusation was there for him to see, and I wanted him to. In case I denied his request, the asshole had gone behind my back and recruited me to help find his mother through the alpha. It really was a shitty thing to do, and I wanted to kick myself for even considering trusting the damn manipulator for even a second. What better way to fish for information about an abusive angel than asking a demon about it?

The plan was perfect.

He'd betrayed the fragile truce we had, but his plan had been top notch, I'd give him that.

He had the decency to flinch at my cold smile. "I'll do it." My words were for the alpha, yet I didn't look away from River. "Fetch us a demon, Alex, and let's get to the bottom of things once and for all."

"Consider it done." The shifter breathed a sigh of relief, but Danika eyed River and me shrewdly.

"If we are done here, I'd like to return to my room. I'm still a little dizzy from the blood loss." Amber and Sissily stiffened, their attention intently locking on me. They knew the tea had fixed everything, and that meant I'd lied. With everything in me, I hoped River would call me out on it, but he kept his trap shut.

"Of course." As I expected, Alex rushed to send me back to bed.

I was too pissed to feel guilty about what I'd done, so with a forced smile, I moseyed out of the office. Danika tracked me but didn't say goodbye, much to my delight. It seemed like a perfectly good day for burning bridges, and I'd done a number on two already. Hopefully, I'd reached the limit for the day.

The door closed behind me with a finality that chilled me to the bone.

Chapter Twenty-Four

Sitting cross-legged in the middle of the bed, I stared at the thick leather tome in front of me. Betrayal burned a hole in my chest, but I ground my teeth, refusing to allow the tears that prickled the back of my eyes to fall. I'd be damned before I shed one tear for that jerk. I should've expected it, yet I dumbly let myself believe that something would change if I tried hard enough. What a dumbass.

People sucked. Big time.

Supernatural and human alike.

Maybe at some point through the history of the human realm there were more who believed in honor, loyalty, and connection. Being honest and kind to one another without any motivation or ulterior motive. As time passed, the number had dwindled until finding one of those people was equivalent to finding a talking cat riding a purple unicorn. In my world, apart from Sissily, and now Alex and Amber, everyone else had some hidden agenda pushing them toward me. They needed to use me for something.

River thought he'd jump ahead of the line and corner

me so I couldn't say no. What was sad was the fact that I'd almost told him I'd do it, actually. So, the joke was on me.

My fingertips grazed the ancient book, and I gently flipped it open. Empty pages met my eyes, but that didn't stop me. One by one, I turned each page, inspecting them thoroughly as if the secrets were hidden in whatever adhesive was used to hold it together. The thick, yellowed paper rasped over my skin with each flick of my wrist, the sound as soothing as the smell of dust and aged ink coming from it.

The alpha's voice bloomed in my mind and pulled me back to a day not that long past, though it felt like it was three lifetimes ago.

"What does this tell you?" Alex thumped a fist over his solar plexus. Sissily hummed something under her nose, but I ignored her.

"That I had too many espressos and I might have a heart attack?" My voice raised a pitch, and the comment turned into a question.

The alpha narrowed his eyes on me dangerously.

Blowing out a breath, I closed my eyes and breathed deeply. Shoulders slumped, I pushed the hum of voices to the back of my mind and focused on my intuition. It was a guide any witch would follow, but mine was barely a whisper from the lack of magic. It was the main reason I never trusted it, but I was willing to humor him.

I didn't expect the stab of fear and the danger alarm to make me rock back on the chair when I did find it. My chair would've toppled over if Alex didn't snatch me by the upper arm to steady me.

"Danger is definitely coming." With great effort, I pushed the words out through numb lips. Sissily stayed silent, but her face looked paler than it already was.

"This is a good thing, little witch." The shifter looked proud like I'd just discovered the Americas.

"Maybe to you. I personally would love it if danger stayed away from me, thank you very much. I have no magic, or did you forget

that?" *I should buy his son some chew toys or something, because if anyone else talked like that to the alpha, he would be playing dodgeball with their head by now.*

I tensed, expecting him to bark at me or something.

Alex threw his head back, and a booming laugh shot out of him.

Sissily and I blinked dumbly at the guffawing shifter.

"A smart predator is a prepared predator, little witch. And you don't need magic to deal with anything life throws at you. I've seen you fight," *The alpha told me when he was done laughing in my face, reminding me of the time I knocked one of his shifters on his ass after he sniffed me.* *"You lose your life when danger finds you suddenly and catches you from a blind spot. If you expect it, the chances of survival are great."*

"I'll keep that in mind."

And that was the reason I was reading empty pages in the middle of the bed like an idiot. Back in his office, intentionally or not, Alex had reminded me of that day. I took his advice and blew up half the coven building, but I had obviously never learned the lesson. Here I was trying to be an informed predator. Snorting laughter escaped my clenched jaw.

I closed my eyes and focused on the intuition that usually evaded me, hoping beyond hope that somehow I'd get a head start on the situation. The tingle started so faintly that I didn't notice it until I was beyond saving my dumb ass. My palm pressed on the open page of the book, and warmth gushed in a wave from it to me. It lit me up from the inside, and I could see the bright golden glow blinding me through my closed eyelids, but I couldn't open them.

Whispers started gaining in volume until they were screaming in my head, and something hot and sticky trickled from my nose and ears. Distantly, I was aware I was bleeding and nothing good ever came from blood pouring from the ears, yet I sat as motionless as a stone statue in the middle of the bed. Frustration gnawed at me because, all this time, the cursed book had remained blank and silent, only to choose now to kill me when I made the executive decision to fight back with every weapon available to me. I thought that was what I'd been doing the whole time, but I was wrong.

Determination was a living thing inside of me.

"Stop!" I shrieked at the overwhelming voices, and they abruptly cut off. "I can't understand a word if you are screaming them inside my brain." There was a great chance I was mentally unstable. Nobody ended well when they spoke to voices in their head, but I was beyond caring at that time.

"What is it you need, child?" Multiple voices spoke at the same time, although at a bearable tone. "Release the barrier you hold between us and let us aid you. Tell us what you want."

"Right. Because I'm an idiot for everything else, so I'll just give you a free-for-all buffet since you asked nicely." I was getting the hang of it with the internal conversation. "Who are you? Better yet, what are you since you are coming from a demonic book?"

My plan was to see if I could communicate with the book that had caused my downfall because I believed it belonged to the demons. If I could ask questions and get it to respond, maybe I could get answers about who is so hell bent on getting their hands on me and where I could find River's mother. As far as insanity went, it was as solid as a rock. So I thought, anyway.

"Demonic?" the voices hissed in disgust. "We belong to no realm, to no living being. All of it belongs to us."

Pounding came from my locked door, and someone's

muffled voice kept calling my name. Tough luck if they thought I'd be opening that door. Blood kept pouring from my face and down the sides of my neck. The way I kept bleeding, Sissily would need a truck full of the grass juice to keep me alive. Hysterical laughter bubbled in my chest.

"I find it hard to believe," I told the book. Or was it the voices? "I think you are killing me by the way. Good luck chatting to the next schmuck who gets screwed by touching your book."

They said they were not demonic. That made them useless to me, so I did what I did best. I sassed them and talked smack. If I pissed them off, I might die faster.

One could only hope.

"You fear us when you should not. Your lifeblood is leaking because you fight what comes natural to you now that we've removed the seal. Give in, child. Let us guide you."

The pounding turned into the door rattling on its hinges. Whoever it was, they were trying to break it in. For a moment, I thought it would be nice if they came to help me get out of whatever place the book had dragged me, but the feeling passed. My body was clammy, cold, and numb.

"Who the fuck are you to guide me?" I'd die talking shit. Just how I liked it. I'd miss Sissily, though. Very much.

The wooden door burst into a shrapnel of splinters that ripped over my skin. I didn't feel the pain from it, just the dull pressure as they passed or entered my flesh. Warm hands plucked me from the bed, and the contact my palm had with the book broke. Before it did, however, I heard what the voices said, and whatever blood I had left turned into ice.

"We are the Fates."

The connection broke. The heaviness to my limbs plunged me into darkness. And what did I do?

I cursed all the way down, calling the voices every name under the sun. I changed my mind about dying. I wanted to interrogate demons. I wanted to help Alex figure everything out. And I even wanted to help that jerk River find his mother.

Most of all, I didn't want to leave Sissily. My friend acted tough, but she was as fragile as a glass figurine. She needed my bitch face to bark at anyone who came close to hurting her. I refused to be gone.

If I never woke up, I'd be pissed as hell.

Please Hecate. Let me wake up.

Next in the Chronicles of Forbidden Witchery Series

vinci-books.com/witchplease

Some witches get a fairy tale—I got a babysitter and a death sentence.

Surviving Death should've earned me a break, but instead, I'm stuck with a womanizing protector and a mess only an archdemon can fix. Vampires, shifters, and scorned lovers want me dead, but I've got one thing to say—*Witch, please.*

Turn the page for a free preview…

Witch Please: Chapter One

I watched everyone around me with a morbid sort of detachment because all I could offer them was some clumsy commiseration thanks to my miserable existence.

Okay fine, I pitied the fools.

They needed to be included in my wretchedness anyway and what better way to accomplish that than to feel sorry for them.

The voices coming from the book announcing they were the Fates rang like a gong in my mind's ear on repeat and nothing could compare to that insanity. Apparently, who we were created to be was pretty much dead and gone from this world we lived in, as I was told. Women simply weren't as healing, nurturing, and soft as they used to be. Men in return weren't as courageous, honorable, and as strong as they used to be. It's the degradation of a system based on ego and rigid intellectual coldness.

It's the devolution of humanity.

And where humanity went, supernaturals followed, of

course. Far be it from us to stay behind some pathetic humans. 'Am I right?

All of it was happening because we lost the inner values. We slammed the door shut to spirit.

We got lost.

That's what the voices in my head were screaming from the top of their lungs twenty-four-seven. The bloody bastards!

You must have a reverence for the divine feminine, they told me. You must have a reverence for the divine masculine. You must have a code of honor. Inner power is the ability to maintain that honor which then opens the mystical doorways to the Spirit. And only this can lead you home.

Apparently, only this will allow me to use my ancestral magic which according to my insanity was the answer to everything.

The voices were persistent, I'd give them that.

Good for them.

Not that I had any intention of listening to the nonsense. I personally wanted to find the nearest bar, so I could get plastered.

I was in desperate need of high quality (I still have standards), strong booze.

The one that you'd feel burning down your throat for days after you've recovered from the hangover and the imprint of the toilet seat on your hands from hugging it tightly is long gone.

Call it what you may but getting piss ass drunk for the night and forgetting everything and everyone for just a moment sounded delightful to me. Maybe better than shopping therapy, if I was being honest.

Okay fine, that's a lie. Nothing is better than shopping,

but getting hammered came in second to best in my humble opinion.

I had every intention of making it happen, too.

"Black?" Sissily tucked a hanger with a silky black blouse under her chin. "Or blue?" A second one replaced the first, the indigo kami swaying gently around her torso with the movement.

"Why do they both look familiar?" My eyes narrowed on her face when her expression changed from thoughtful to one of shock with a comical widening of her eyes. She tried to recover quickly; I had to be proud of her for that but there was no way I'd let her get away with it. "Both came from my closet, didn't they?"

"You haven't touched these in at least a year and a half, they were getting depressed and lonely, from being shunned in the deep dark recesses at the back of your closet." My friend muttered defensively, and she wasn't ready to let this go. "If I remember correctly, and these are your words not mine, you wouldn't be seen dead in something so last season." Her peepers rolled to the back of her head playfully and I couldn't stop my lips from curling up.

I was giving her a hard time just to have fun. The woman was wearing additional clothing on her person to cover my clumsy ass every time I needed to replace what I was wearing. I had no right to complain even if she took every piece of fabric I owned. Designer or otherwise.

"And you thought I'd be willing to be seen with you wearing something so last season?" My arched eyebrow was answered with a derisive snort. "I didn't think so."

"I figured I'd at least make an effort, since you are very adamant about going out. I'm sure I'll never hear the end of it if I try to step out of the room in a t-shirt." Tossing both hangers on the armchair with a huff, she threw herself onto the bed next to me. "Why can't we just go grab a couple," she saw my scowl and amended the ridiculous statement immediately. "A few actually, now that I think about it, bottles of wine or gin, and bring them here? We can get perfectly drunk in Pj's, too. No need for fancy clothing or makeup. Get what I mean? It'll be comfy as all hell, as well."

"If I stay in this room for another hour, I'm going to self-combust, Sissily." It was not an exaggeration of the truth, and she knew it. "The longer we mingle, the more I have an urge to jump out of my skin, claw my ears off, or poke out my eyeballs. Can we just go?"

"You sure we will be good to leave the house?" Sissily queried, trying and epically failing to hide the worry creasing the corners of her eyes, she rolled off the bed and stood up. "Friend or not, Alex gives me the heebie-jeebies every time he focuses on me."

"Yeah, he knows we are going to the pub for a drink. He owns the place after all it's not like we can hide on pack lands." Following her example, I stood too and started searching for my shoes while pretending the lightheadedness was not there. "I was very clear that I will either go or his home might blow up like Danika's coven building. You should see how fast he agreed."

"I bet he did." Snickering under her breath as if the alpha was standing on the other side of my closed door, waiting to hear if she would say something bad about him, she was almost gleeful when she turned to face me. "We can totally get anything we want if we use you as a threat like that."

"Oh yeah?" Noticing the heel poking out from under a pile of dirty clothing next to the dresser, I shook my head at her as I bent over to pick it up. "And what would you…"

Whatever else was about to come out of my mouth was forgotten when dizziness made me tip over to the side and my whole-body weight slammed into the drawers of the tall dresser. The few decorations and the group of three vases perched on top of it rattled loudly, one of the glass tubes smacking hard on the wood and rolling off of it to shatter on the parquet floor at my feet. My stomach rolled from the bile that churned inside it as numbness spread through my limbs followed by a cold sweat which drenched my tank top in no time.

"Hazel!" Sissily was next to me so fast I would've flinched when she grabbed me by the shoulders if I could. "Hazel, talk to me girl. What's wrong?"

I must give credit to Sissily. For a tiny little thing the woman was strong. She bodily carried me back to the bed where she dropped me like some poorly chosen prom dress, she regretted buying. All I could do was breathe through my nose and press my lips tight in case the acid burning inside me decided to erupt violently, but I watched her while she frantically turned this way and that not knowing what to do. Suddenly she spun on her heel and rushed to the door that she proceeded to yank open hard enough to make the frame groan.

"Alex!" my friend bellowed from the top of her lungs. The silent house met her shout. "Amber! Hazel needs help!"

As if she used a magic word the emptiness of the home became a cacophony of sound with people calling out to each other and a few pairs of feet came running across the floor in our direction. Remembering the conversation, I had with the alpha a couple of hours earlier I almost laughed. The poor male thinks I'm about to redecorate his home and is probably debating if he should toss me out the window just in case.

"Where is she?"

My heart stopped at the sound of the deep baritone and all the blood drained from my head. My mind was screaming no but there was absolutely nothing I could do to stop the clusterfuck that was about to unfold. To make matters worse, I watched mortified as River rushed to my side and gathered my limp, sweat soaked body in his arms.

"What happened? The pack is taking up positions around the house as a double protection." Blondie looked sharply at my friend who hovered over me like a mother hen, wringing his hands.

"Speak female!"

"Don't you yell at me River Blackman." Sassily hissed at him, getting in his face and if I could, I would've kissed the girl. Good for her telling the jerk off. I mean who died and made him one of the gods? "If I knew do you think I'd be shouting for help like an idiot? One moment she was mocking me about last season's fashion and bent over to pick up her shoe, the next she dropped like a rock pale as a ghost."

"Hazel, can you hear me?" Rough fingers rasped over the skin on my forehead as he brushed hair out of my face. "Does anything hurt? Blink once if you can't talk." Sissily's face popped above me crinkled with worry. "At least she's not bleeding, that's a good thing." River muttered to himself.

"Security is tight around the house. Is she hurt?" Alex rushed into the room filling it up with potent alpha energy strong enough to pebble my skin. "Is she breathing?" His worried face joined my friend above me and all I could do was stare at both of them.

No sound was coming out of me anytime soon. A strange tingling sensation started on my lips and slowly spread all over my face and body, but it did nothing but remind me I was not dead, at least not yet at any rate. At least it wasn't unpleasant or painful; and with my experiences lately everyone was all hellbent on killing me. I was grateful for that.

"Should I call for a healer?" Alex turned his mismatched gaze to River as if blondie held the knowledge of what would help me.

"I think she can hear us but for whatever reason she can't talk." Sissily reached a hand out and yanked on my right eyelid, lifting it up to expose most of my eyeball. In front of Blackman.

The woman was mental.

Lucky for her I couldn't slap her. I made a note to do it as soon as I regained movement to my limbs. The tingling was getting stronger at that point, so with Hecate's help I'd be smacking her any time now. The thought made me giddy with excitement; it also distracted me enough to avoid a panic attack. You'd think I'd be used to this shit by now but no. I was still quaking in my designer shoes every minute of every day expecting to drop where I stood for no reason at all.

It was the story of my life now.

Thank you, stupid magic.

And to think I was begging any gods who listened or the universe to grant me the wish of having power like the rest of my kind. No wonder humans said be careful what you wish for, you just might get it.

The pentagram on the side of my forefinger started burning strong enough that the harsh breath I sucked in sounded like a hiss.

"She's coming around." Sissily took my hand in hers and gave it a reassuring squeeze before dropping it like it bit her. "Oh, dear Hecate, her skin is burning up." Her blue peepers turned accusingly to River. "Why are you sitting there mute, Blackman? You waiting to see if she catches on fire?"

"She's cool to the touch." A line formed between his eyebrows as he searched my face for discomfort was my guess. The fingers of one of his hands glided over my arm raising goosebumps on my skin. "Unless…"

Blessed reprieve came when he took my hand in his, where his skin connected with my burning flesh. The tears which were gathering in the corners of my eyes were gone too and the tingling sensation faded as well. That was my cue to get away from him because it seemed like he knew that he could help remove the pain I was experiencing.

The last thing I needed was to owe Blackman anything.

"I'm okay." I rasped out on a deep breath as soon as my tongue felt less thick in my mouth. "I'm fine." My attempt to push away from River so I can place distance between us, as expected, failed miserably. I only managed to flop around like a fish out of water rubbing myself all over his lap. Speaking of which, "I just need some water." I told no one in particular but they stared at me like I suddenly grew a second head. "…Please?" I added lamely after a long awkward pause raising the pitch of my tone just enough to make it a question.

God forbid anyone mistakes me for a polite individual.

"She's dying." Sissily wailed taking fistfuls of Alex's shirt in a white-knuckled grip.

"Ha, ha. Very funny." Grumbling under my breath, I kept up my attempt to dislodge River. "I've barely eaten anything today so that must be the reason for the dizziness. Nothing a few burgers and a handful of desserts can't fix."

Alex was already nodding and pulling his phone out of the back pocket of his jeans. Dejectedly, I watched my escape for the night die a sudden death when the alpha ordered a ton of food to be brought up to my room. Any chance of getting plastered went down the drain with it unless I could convince Sissily to go get a few bottles as she earlier suggested. My gaze narrowed on my friend's face, and she returned the favor already reading my expression that I was contemplating something.

In all the scrutiny I was giving my friend, River's hand slipped under my tank top from the wiggling I was doing turning me into a stone statue when I became as stiff as a board. "For Hecate's sake Blackman, you are like a damn octopus. Keep those tentacles to yourself would ya?"

He took mercy on me and released me finally with a maddening smirk on his face. Sissily didn't help matters with the couple of snorts she was trying her best to cover up with a cough. Even Alex was hiding a grin by rubbing a hand over his mouth.

"I'm glad I can amuse all of you." Twisting my lips to show my displeasure, I plopped onto the mattress and blew at the strand of hair that fell over my face. That's when this whole thing took a turn toward a clusterfuck of epic proportions.

"River?" came a soft feminine voice from the open door of my room.

You could hear a pin drop.

We all turned to find a rather attractive blonde with big emerald eyes smiling shyly at Blackman. A sharp pain speared me in the center of the chest that I pretended I didn't notice, and I forced my mouth to stretch into a smile while glancing at my friend. Sissily shook her head sharply to tell me I probably looked hideous, so I dropped the expression immediately.

"I'm sorry, I didn't know you were busy." The pretty blonde blinked at River so seductively even I wanted to go shove my tongue down her throat. "I'll see you later." She turned to leave but as always, I was a glutton for punishment.

Everyone kept their mouth shut, even River. Did I do that as well, you ask?

No.

Have you met me? Of course, I wanted to make him feel as awful as I felt. If I had to suffer, so should he, the insufferable bastard!

"Who's your friend, River?" My chirpy tone made Sissily groan as if in pain.

"I think I'm developing a headache too." My bestie told the alpha who was rubbing his temples and shaking his head at Blackman.

"What?" My innocent question didn't fool anyone, not even me, and it made a muscle spasm in River's jaw.

Seriously. Sometimes you just can't win against people.

Lesson 18: *Everything is fair in love and war, unless you are a witch. It's like a train wreck; you are cringing but can't force yourself to look away.*

I butchered the hell out of everything, and obviously I butchered any chances of love coming my way, too.

Witch Please: Chapter Two

"I don't understand why I can't ask a simple question without it turning into a pack drama." I told Sissily as I stuffed a handful of fries in my mouth. "Isf wuf ouf of pofuftnes." My chipmunk cheeks puffed out as I tried to talk with a mouthful before swallowing the food half chewed in my urgency to argue my case. "It was out of politeness." I repeated in case she misunderstood my food filled sentence earlier as I wiped the grease from my mouth with the back of my hand.

According to Alex and Sissily, I was being an ass and making River's life miserable. To which I disagreed wholeheartedly. "I can be polite you know. What?" She was about to roll her eyes I could feel it, but my glare made her think better of it. "I can."

"You?" Sissily leaned back and looked at me up and down before nodding thoughtfully. "You can totally be polite and very nice." My smile full of gratitude was as premature as Mike's ejaculation according to the stories my bestie had told me. "You just chose to be rude."

Well, she wasn't wrong about that. I did choose to be rude, but I had my reasons for that, damn it.

"Anywhoooo," picking the pickle out of my burger I slapped it on the plate with disgust. A shiver ran up and down my spine as I fished between the buns for more of the yucky things. "I wasn't trying to be rude or mean. I was honestly curious about who the bombshell was. Weren't you?"

The mumble coming out of my bestie was the buzzing of a mosquito and it abruptly cut off when my hand froze with my fingers in the burger up to the second knuckle and my eyes narrowed dangerously on her face.

"I'm sorry, what?" It was so unusual to watch Sissily squirm that I almost dropped the burger in my lap.

"I said," on a deep exhale, she deflated like a balloon looking all dejected and shit. "I've seen him talking to her a few times while you were recovering from the last blood loss. I was hoping to avoid you seeing it though."

"Why?" recovering my food I took a huge bite and chewed thoughtfully while watching her like a hawk. "You think I care who River talks to?" Genuinely puzzled, I finally asked when I swallowed the bite.

"You don't?" Sissily challenged with one eyebrow arrowed up.

No was on the tip of my tongue but since my bestie rarely sassed me about males, I took a deep breath and examined my thoughts and feelings on the matter. Life was crappy as it was without taking things too seriously; so, we both acted immature on most days to offset the stress we faced. Occasionally though we had to be adults.

"I am a hot-blooded female, Sissily. It would be a lie if I said I don't think about jumping Blackman's bones at least three times a day. I have a vagina." Both eyebrows raised, I pointed to my crotch in case she didn't know where the organ was located. "That being said I rather he stays away from me as far as possible; so, him talking to other females is a good thing."

There. I could be an adult. Don't look at me like that! I could!

Neither Sissily, nor I for that matter believed a word coming out of my mouth.

"I can always zap her and burn her hair to a crisp." Sissily offered conversationally while plucking layers of flaky dough from the croissant she's been gnawing on the last twenty minutes. "No one looks good with a typhus hairstyle. I bet she won't look good then."

I snorted despite myself.

"You're so stupid."

"Genius you mean?"

"That, too." Returning her smile, I continued eating because I really hated the fact I couldn't get out of the damn room and get plastered because of dizziness from lack of nourishment. With everything going on, I would forget to eat on most days unless someone reminds me. Amber was mothering the hell out of me but with the increase of attacks on pack lands the poor female could barely remember her own name.

Howls sounded from outside, loud enough to be heard crystal clear in my room. Another reminder that thanks to me no one was safe. And here I was dwelling on River's love life instead of facing my own crap. As if sensing the direction of my thoughts, or maybe my faraway gaze aimed at the window was an indication, Sissily reassuringly squeezed my arm.

"We will figure things out eventually." She muttered like she was scared to say it too loud and tempt fate.

Speaking of which...

"What do you suppose it means?" my bestie knew exactly who I was referring to without me voicing it. "It could be a demonic trick."

I still refused to accept the fact that the cursed book was somehow a portal for communicating with the Fates. The way the demons have been attacking every chance they get and recruiting the rest of the supernaturals, I wouldn't put it pass them to try trickery. It was their very nature after all. No one could blame a snake for biting them. It's a snake, it's what they do.

Same with demons.

Unless they try to eat your designer shirt. That shit is simply unheard of.

Sissily lifted her face and made a loud sniffing sound. My frown made her grin at me like a fiend. "I can smell something burning. You are trying to use your brain, huh? Don't think too hard it'll short circuit."

I kicked at her, or at least I tried halfheartedly to kick her, I should say. Her giggle was short-lived and cut off when the second set of howls nearly shook the house with its intensity. After a few seconds of staring at each other owlishly, we scrambled off the bed and raced toward the curtain covered window.

Parting the thick fabric slightly, I did my best to see in the pitch black what was going on with one eye. Sissily was doing the same on the other side, her breath seesawing in the silence of the room but I doubt she was having any better luck. It seemed that someone plunged the grounds around the large home into darkness and only an occasional eerie glow of predatory eyes broke it. Luckily those I saw all belonged to the wolves.

"Something is going on out there." Sissily said, her voice trembling from the adrenaline I too was experiencing.

"You think?" craning my neck and pressing my forehead harder to the glass where my nose was squished sideways, I snorted at her. "No shit, Sherlock." My breath fogged up the window, and I missed if it was a wolf looking up at where we were or if it was something else.

"You're such a jerk." My bestie groused, pouting at me from the other side of the window when I looked her way.

"I'm going." Not allowing her time to process what I said, I rushed around the room and hurriedly stabbed my feet into the flattest boots I could find. They ended up having a two-inch heel but better than a stiletto, I guess.

"Like I thought you'd do something else, Hazel. You do remember I've known you since we were kids, right?"

A shrill scream rattled the windows, and I made a mad dash toward it yanking on the curtain without a second thought. We were beyond the point of hiding. Whoever was out there didn't care to stay hidden anymore, so I didn't see why I should be hiding either. After all, I was pretty sure they were here for me. Sissily stepped up next to me as we gazed down into the darkness of the back yard.

A shadow slithered between two shrubs, their leaves rusting from the disturbance, but they were too fast for my eyes to track. A few of the clouds parted at that moment thankfully allowing the partial moon to illuminate the yard long enough that I was able to identify the usurper. My heart skipped a beat before stuttering into a rapid-fire rhythm.

"Mazzikin." Sissily and I said at the same time as we locked gazes.

Mazzikin is not a specific type of demon from Hell specifically, but rather they are a broad classification of a range of evil spirits in the same way we see demons. They are the cheeky little blighters of the demon hierarchy, maddeningly irritating and hard to get a hold of. They are as pesky as the imps who are permanently armed with the spanners that so often get thrown into the works but more vicious when it comes to harming supernaturals. In short, Mazzikin are mean little critters, or invisible types of demons, who cause everyday stressors and tribulations for humans. The problem was, wherever these little buggers showed up, much bigger problems followed for those like me.

There was only one way to get rid of the Mazzikin and luckily for the pack, Danika being her typical self and tormenting me with useless knowledge was about to pay off big time.

"Let's go." I snatched my bestie by the hand and yanked her along with me through the door and out into the hallway. It was as empty as a tomb which was expected with all the fighting and howling going on outside. "I know what to do."

"You do?" Sissily panted as we took the stairway down two stairs at a time.

Yes, I do." Gasping for air, as well, I sped up. "Mazzikin are spirits, Sissily. What's the easiest way to get rid of them from this plane of existence? Think."

"Hazel! I could kiss you right now." She squealed and redoubled her efforts to get downstairs before me now that she knew what we should do to end the nightmare before someone gets seriously hurt. "Remember though, if Danika asks, we know nothing."

"I'd die before I say a word." I told her solemnly. "We don't need additional things for her to hold over our heads."

The very thought of my grandmother had my blood

boiling, but I pushed it down in order to focus on what we had to do. Reaching the front double doors, I took a hold of the ornate knobs and yanked both open at the same time just as Sissily breezed past me and skidded to a stop within a few feet.

Shifters raced around on four and two legs, shouts and howls echoing in the night. My heart stuttered when I noticed the flickering images of the shades start gathering closer to where the two of us joined the skirmish. I knew they were sent here for me even without the obvious signs.

"We should start now..." Sissily was saying but I waved a hand at her to cut her off and pointed at the cluster of shrubs to the left where two wolves were snapping their jaws at one of the Mazzikin.

"We should wait a little just to be jerks." My grin made her glare at me. "What? He is a know it all, isn't he?" We watched River dance around the shade, his magic passing through it without making a scratch. "This will teach him a lesson."

Dark eyes locked on my gloating face and narrowed with suspicion. I wondered for a split second if he heard me and that's why he didn't rush to play my guardian, but every thought left the moment a few of the demons beelined for Sissily.

All the blood drained from my head when I realized she was looking at me over her shoulder and didn't see them coming. She was a few feet ahead of me, so they were much closer to her, and I had no chance of reaching her before they did.

"Duck!" My scream had her dropping like a rock, face first onto the concrete path. Blondie was yelling something too, but I blocked him out completely. "Roll!"

My feet were already moving when Sissily rolled toward me avoiding one of the shades that dove for the spot where she prostrated herself. Sprinting, I bent down as I reached my friend and snatched her up by the arm. She twisted easily, more from years of sparring together than intuition or anything else and pushed herself off of the ground. My momentum helped us both keep our balance and we raced for the line of trees where we could find shelter for a few seconds.

Many howls sounded around us pebbling my skin.

Fear clawed at my insides, guilt drilling a hole in my gut. My petty nature almost cost Sissily her sanity. If any of the Mazzikin possesses a witch, she or he would lose their mind. There was no returning from that.

As we reached the few trees, I slammed my back onto one of the trunks pulling Sissily with me. We both gasped loudly, sucking in air for our starved lungs more out of panic than for being out of shape. Although that damn burger was trying to come up a couple of times since I left the safety of my room.

"Ready?" I panted. "We gotta do it now."

She just nodded spastically while blowing air through her nostrils like a bull.

"*Exorcizamus te, omnis...*" a coughing fit had me doubling over and I almost lost the food I stuffed in my mouth earlier all over the leaf covered ground.

"Hazel!" River's shout had my heart punching the roof of my mouth and without turning to see where he was yelling from, I dropped on the ground pulling Sissily with me.

The short hairs on the back of my neck lifted to attention when I felt the soft tickling breeze from the shade that missed me by a hair.

"Sissily?" My gasp was followed by spitting out leaves that filled my mouth when I faceplanted.

"Start." Anger colored her tone, and she squeezed my hand hard enough to grind my bones. I knew exactly how she felt because I was starting to get pissy, too.

"Exorcizamus te, omnis immundus spiritus, omnis satanica potestas, omnis incursio infernalis adversarii, omnis legio, omnis congregatio et secta diabolica."

Our voices rose with each word but as we finished the chant, oppressive silence formed a vacuum between my ears. Sissily and I looked at each other, both of us wide-eyed and covered in dirt. I could see clear as day the doubt written all over her face if we did this right or if we miscalculated the situation completely.

You could hear a pin drop.

And that's when the shrieks started loud enough to make my ears bleed.

Cursed demons and their penchant for draining the blood from my body.

Grab your copy...
vinci-books.com/witchplease

About the Author

Maya Daniels, USA Today Bestselling and multi-award-winning supernatural suspense author, is a fun-loving woman with many talents.

She traveled the world, gaining life experiences that helped her career as an investigative journalist, as well as her storytelling. Maya writes compelling tales of magic, mythical creatures, loyalty, and life-changing friendships with snarky female characters—much like herself.

Her travels have taken her to Europe, Africa, Asia, Australia, and America. Born with her feet in motion, she currently resides in Ohio, spinning her next epic story that you will not want to put down.

Her biggest 'sins' are her love of chocolate and coffee—through an IV drip! One to never sit still, Maya practices Reiki healing, different types of martial arts, reads about the arcane, talks to furry creatures more than humans, picks up a sledgehammer for home improvement, and travels with her fated mate, seeking her own adventures.

www.ingramcontent.com/pod-product-compliance
Ingram Content Group UK Ltd.
Pitfield, Milton Keynes, MK11 3LW, UK
UKHW040405140426
469799UK00009B/122